WINTER GRAVES

A DR HARRISON LANE MYSTERY
BOOK 7

GWYN BENNETT

Storm

Ebook ISBN: 978-1-80508-005-3
Paperback ISBN: 978-1-80508-006-0

Cover design: Tash Webber
Cover images: Alamy (RF), Shutterstock

Published by Storm Publishing.
For further information, visit:
www.stormpublishing.co

ALSO BY GWYN BENNETT

The Dr Harrison Lane Mysteries

1. *Broken Angels*

2. *Beautiful Remains*

3. *Deadly Secrets*

4. *Innocent Dead*

5. *Perfect Beauties*

6. *Captive Heart*

7. *Winter Graves*

8. *Dark Whispers*

The DI Clare Falle Series

1. *Lonely Hearts*

2. *Home Help*

3. *Death Bond*

The Villagers

1

DECEMBER 16TH

They waited and watched. Waited for the light beams on the tall church spire to turn off, and the bright Christmas illuminations to go dark. Watched, ensuring there was nobody left inside the building.

It was time. 11 p.m. on the dot. The night enveloped the church and its grounds. It would be difficult for any passer-by to see them as they slipped up the path towards the side entrance. The moon and stars were smothered by clouds. The sky a big black hole. That suited them just fine.

They walked, a shadow, head bowed, through the dark graveyard. Dressed all in black from head to toe. A long black coat, black leather gloves. A black scarf across their face.

Despite its midnight hue, their clothing didn't look out of place that cold winter's night. The wind was biting. A northerly that was due to bring snow before the week was out. It was the kind of wind which made the bushes shiver and seemed capable of turning water to ice with just one breath.

They weren't interested in the weather, though it had kept

others indoors. There was just one thing on the intruder's mind. In their left hand they carried a bag which sloshed and clunked as they strode up the path, feet scrunching on the gravel in accompaniment. It had some tools, a heavy-duty garden refuse sack, and a can of diesel inside. In their right hand was a set of keys. They wouldn't need to break in to enter.

The dark figure's eyes darted around the churchyard. Had they seen movement in the shadows? They stopped, stilling their feet on the gravel. Listening intently and scanning every inch of the graveyard. Every headstone. Every mawkish religious monument to the departed. Their eyes had grown accustomed to the lack of light.

There it was again. A movement to the left. They tensed. Excuses had been well rehearsed should they bump into anyone, and so they ran through the lines quickly in their head.

Then they saw a pair of green eyes staring back and, with an annoyed flick of its tail, a black cat slipped away behind a gravestone.

The intruder let out a breath of relief and finished the last few steps to the church door. They tried several keys before feeling the lock give way and the rotor slide round. Within seconds, they'd slipped inside.

Behind them, the graveyard returned to the sole ownership of the dead.

They knew where the silver was kept, locked away in the sacristy. They'd toyed with the idea of taking it, making the whole thing look like a robbery, but that would have defeated one objective. They needed to make a clear statement. Let the others know they were coming for them. They wanted fear to find its way into their hearts and souls. A fear that couldn't be quenched by their religion. A fear begotten from a sin that could never be forgiven.

It was dark inside the church and the intruder couldn't turn on the lights in case someone saw them. They fumbled in the bag for the head torch they'd brought and pulled it over the top of their black hat. When they were sure it was firmly in place, they switched it on, sending a beam of white light out in front of them. The light illuminated the pulpit with its Christmas tree sentinels and holly decorations, sending shadows leering up the surrounding walls. They had no fear of this place. Only hatred.

They took the can of diesel out of the bag and left it on the front pew. Then moved down the aisle, heading for the door tucked away on the left side. Few noticed this door. It was old and small, requiring most people of modern height to duck in order to go through. It was also kept locked. This was not a door for the congregation to enter. Not a place that most people would want to visit. Behind that door were stone steps down into the bowels of the church, where the rich and the privileged spent eternity waiting for the revelation.

The intruder tried a few of the keys on the ring before finally finding the right one. The lock didn't give as easily as the church's side door had. It was rarely used, but eventually it surrendered. The door squeaked on its hinges when pushed open, a sound which seemed to fill the big flint stone church as though calling out a warning to its guardians. Its efforts would go to waste.

The head torch illuminated the narrow flight of stone steps descending into the darkness and highlighted the dust motes which floated away in the breeze of the door opening. Tiny orbs which guided them downwards.

The air was musty and stagnant. Occupants of this chamber didn't need to breathe, and there was no ventilation to circulate and freshen the atmosphere. The corridor was narrow, only just wide enough to fit a coffin down – as long as you weren't a large corpse.

As the intruder walked along, they passed sealed chambers with ancient name plaques announcing the residents. Lord and Lady Weston, who had passed in the late 1800s. Sir Robert Mackenzie, who had apparently served his God, King, and country before making his final journey through the floor of the church and into the crypt. The intruder wasn't interested in any of them.

They pressed forward into a large open area at the end, where coffins lay on stone shelves around a horseshoe-shaped chamber. Somewhere among these unsuspecting souls lay a devil's corpse. A master con artist who had fooled congregations for decades with his false piety and benevolence. Bishop Peter Warriner, who unfortunately had died before justice could be served on him but would not escape his trial.

Most of the caskets were old, pre-World War Two, so it was easy to spot the modern interloper. Thankfully, it was on the middle shelf. Easy to reach.

They took the tools from the bag. First they tested the lid in case it was unsealed. It didn't move and so they looked for the locking mechanism at the foot. This would need to be turned to release the lid. The older caskets around it had simply been nailed shut. Once the lock had been turned, they steeled themselves for a moment. Covering their mouth and nose with the scarf and taking a few deep breaths, before prising open the lid.

The gagging miasma of formaldehyde and rot seeped out like a stagnant swamp. As it hit them, they stepped back, but the impact was minimal. Their sense of taste and smell had started to disappear a couple of weeks ago and, for once, this misfortune served them well. The bishop had been dead for some time and the decomposition and all its gasses had been trapped inside the sealed coffin. But the intruder was immune to him in death, as well as in life.

They stepped forward to peer inside and were relieved to see the body wasn't a watery mush, but had started to mummify in the dry atmosphere. The skin was brownish-black, his face like a ghastly sunken skull covered in papier-mâché. The body was dressed in the vestments of his clerical rank, a robe with a stole, discoloured by bodily fluids, and a large cross hanging around the neck and resting on the chest.

The intruder took the garden waste sack out of the bag and began to feed the body into it. They had to be careful to avoid the corpse falling apart with barely anything to hold it together, but eventually the earthly remains of Bishop Warriner were inside the bag. They heaved it free, not caring to show any respect.

They could have resealed the casket, barely left a trace of what had actually gone on here, but then it wouldn't send its message. Instead, they took some wire cutters from the bag and looked inside the garden sack for the bishop's right hand. Without any emotion, the desecrator cut three fingers from it and returned the fingers to the casket. The rest of Bishop Warriner, they dragged unceremoniously back up the narrow corridor and into the church, leaving the garden sack by the side door ready to leave.

The intruder returned to the main body of the church and picked up the can of diesel. They began to splash it over the wooden pews where countless sinners had sat, hoping to find guidance and resurrection from a man more flawed than they were. A man who had hidden behind his pulpit and his God and preached at them week after week.

They poured the diesel over the altar cloth, the Christmas

tree, the poinsettia displays, and the wooden nativity scene at the back. The lies and falsehoods of their celebration. Then, one by one, they lit matches and threw them at the diesel. Time after time, relishing the whoosh of blue flame as it caught light. They'd have liked to stand and watch, but they knew the flames and smoke would quickly develop and apart from it not being safe, it would alert people. They had to make their escape. There was still so much to do.

The intruder slipped out the side door with their bag of tools and the garden waste sack, and locked the door behind them. Then they made their way back up the graveyard path, their breathing more laboured with the heavier load. Before they left, they took something from the holdall. It was inside a clear sealed bag, isolated so as not to contaminate it with any of their DNA from the tools.

They knew where the CCTV camera pointed and so stayed close to the wall, hiding in the shadows, before finally reaching the main door to the church. There, they placed the clay doll at the entrance and melted back into the darkness.

As they drove away, the first plumes of grey were beginning to escape and the smoke alarms inside were screeching their warnings. By the time the fire crews arrived, there would be considerable damage. Perhaps it might even spread to the roof. The hypocrisy of their Christian Christmas would have to take place somewhere else.

2

DECEMBER 16TH

Justin Black had been getting himself ready for bed. This was not a long process. Justin liked his routines. He would shower in the morning, ready for the day ahead, and just have a small wash prior to retiring for the night. He liked to have a hot chocolate before bed. Drunk up to an hour prior to sleep in order to ensure that he wasn't going to get up in the night to use the toilet. At just gone sixty, Justin's bladder was not as robust as it had once been.

He'd retired from the clerical job where he'd given the best years of his life, although if he had to be honest in front of the Lord, Justin would admit it was redundancy rather than a conscious decision to leave. The only positive from the whole experience was that his length of service meant he got a nice tidy pay off.

Nowadays, Justin was able to dedicate his time to his community, apart from the part-time role he had at the local supermarket, where he helped with the shelf re-stocking and occasionally worked the tills. The job came with a decent staff discount for his purchases, and so the measly wages he received each week went much further when it came to his weekly shop.

Justin had never found a partner in life. For one thing, it had taken him until his thirties to realise that his lack of attraction to women – which was reciprocated – was down to his inherent low levels of libido and a passing preference for men. Justin was still a virgin and felt no great regret nor need to change that status quo.

His passion, and the main focus of his life, was the Church. Justin had been a choirboy at the village church of All Saints and had continued his dedication throughout his life. He could count on one hand the number of times that he'd missed a Sunday service. One was because he'd come down with the flu, which resulted in two weeks of forced absence, but was made better by a visit from the vicar, who blessed him and gave him strength.

Another time, his mother had been dying in the hospice. The doctors had told him she was unlikely to last the next hour and so he'd stayed with her rather than go to church. He'd held her hand, read passages from the Bible, and prayed. As it turned out, he could have gone. She clung on into the early hours of the next morning and slipped from this world when he'd finally given up and was tucked up in bed at home.

Covid had also put paid to a couple of services, but thankfully the vicar was quick to get up and running with the online alternative and so although he hadn't been able to visit the church with the others, he did at least feel an internet connection to his God.

Justin had lived a 'small' life. No foreign travel, one full-time employer, and he'd never moved further than a stone's throw from the church of All Saints where he'd been baptised. His mother's old cottage had been his home from birth. But he was content, and never more so than in the last few years when he'd become a verger. The role came with responsibilities. He welcomed the congregations in, supported the vicar in the planning of church events, and he helped oversee the sexton with the maintenance of the graveyard and church building. Whatever was required, Justin was always happy to do it.

One of the advantages of his little cottage was that it stood across the road from the church itself. He could see it from his bedroom window, and he often sat in his old armchair in the living room downstairs, looking across at the wooden entrance gate to the graveyard, framed by the grey stone bulk of the nave behind it. If he wanted to see the tower, then that required a bit of contortion, bending forward and looking up and to the left. What mattered was that his church filled the windows of his little home. He couldn't wish for a better view.

It was why, when Justin was just drifting off to sleep in his dark bedroom, the sound of smoke alarms made him jar to attention. His eyes shot open and the black darkness that he'd earlier closed them to was now freckled with orange flickers.

His heart jumped into his throat, and he flung himself out of bed and over to the window. When he drew the curtain back, a howl of pain came from his gut. His beloved church was on fire.

As he pulled on some clothes, shoving his feet into shoes, he called 999 on the small mobile phone he'd bought so that the vicar could keep in touch. He shouted a command to the operator to send the fire brigade to All Saints as quickly as possible and then ended the call. He had no time to chat.

As he ran across the road and into the graveyard, he watched the orange flames dancing and mocking through the nave windows. The Devil's work destroying their beloved church. His hands shook with adrenaline as he found the right key and plunged it into the main door lock. There were fire extinguishers in the entrance. He could use them to keep the flames back while he waited for the fire engines to come.

As he wrenched the doors open, thick black smoke billowed out, making him bend double, coughing. His eyes stung. He felt like vomiting, but he pressed forward.

Justin grabbed the nearest fire extinguisher and pulled its pin out. He'd been on the fire warden course last year. He knew exactly what to do.

What he hadn't been taught, or maybe he'd forgotten, was that opening the big doors into the main building would only fan the fire. Feeding it with fresh oxygen. The wind funnelling through the entranceway spread the sparks and flames, pushing the flames upwards so that they licked at the delicious oak roof struts that had been cut and dried centuries ago.

Justin had God on his side. He was working for the good of his community. For his church. For the one constant that had never failed him in his life. He ran into the smoke, pointing the extinguisher at the wooden pews which were burning like the Guy Fawkes bonfires just weeks before.

When the first canister ran out, he headed back to the entrance for a fresh one. Only the smoke had made him confused. He found himself at the altar. The opposite end of the nave from the exit. The opposite end to where he had expected to be.

Something in his memory told him to get down on the floor and crawl. Keep low. Try to get under the smoke. But the noxious fumes had already poisoned his brain, made his eyes water, and filled his lungs. Even crawling became too much effort and he'd sunk onto the stone floor, coughing and wheezing. His body running out of oxygen.

He made one last effort to try to rise. To save his church. But the beams in the ceiling had started to burn through and rained down large red-hot embers onto his back. His hair and jumper caught light. He was too weak to roll, to put out the flames.

Justin Black died in the epicentre of the blaze. He left this earth with no regrets. He died a hero, attempting to save the one thing he had truly loved in this life. For him, it was his biggest achievement.

3

DECEMBER 17TH

Dr Harrison Lane had fallen asleep to the sound of Mariah Carey's 'All I Want For Christmas Is You', which he'd already heard at least four times that evening. Somebody at the party in the flat downstairs was clearly making a play for a fellow reveller; although Wham's 'Last Christmas' had also been top of the repeat plays, so there was no telling what state their love life was actually in.

Harrison had forgotten about the party. His neighbour had told him a few weeks ago, but it had disappeared in the melee of cases and personal revelations. They had even invited him, despite the fact they'd barely spoken to each other over the years. It wasn't that his neighbour was unsociable, but because their paths had rarely crossed and Harrison had never needed to borrow a cup of sugar or to collect a parcel. He guessed the invite was more to keep him sweet than because they actually wanted to toast Christmas with him. If he was at the party, he couldn't complain about the noise.

He didn't complain. Harrison was so wiped out after a

busy week in Yorkshire that, with the help of the thick indus-trial floorboards separating his Docklands penthouse flat from those below, what noise did leach into his bedroom wasn't sufficient to keep him awake. He just wished that someone would make Mariah's wish come true so she could take a break, too.

His only regret was that he hadn't fallen asleep next to his favourite forensics officer, Dr Tanya Jones. After he'd returned to London, he'd toyed with the idea of heading over to her flat instead of his own, but he was not a man who put his own wishes above the needs of someone else. He was exhausted. If he was going to give his best to the victim of the Suffolk church attack – his latest case and the first in his new job with the National Crime Agency – then sleep was what his tired brain needed.

Instead, he'd made do with a video call and the knowl-edge that in just a week's time they would be spending Christmas Day together. Maybe even Christmas Eve if he played his cards right. It was a pleasant thought to drift off to sleep on.

4

___

DECEMBER 17TH

It was irritating that the investigators had still not discovered Bishop Warriner's corpse was missing. Even more irritating was that the fool verger had decided to try to play hero and managed to barbecue himself and take all the limelight. The outpouring of tributes to Justin Black's dedication and service to his community meant that the message that should have been sent had still not been communicated to those who should be praying to their God for deliverance.

Martin Soulsby, the vicar of St Luke's church, had proven to be a cowardly servant of God. He certainly didn't have the backbone of the All Saints' verger. He'd have sold his own mother if it had meant he didn't have to meet his maker just yet, and suffer pain. He was the second on the list of four.

There were three names written down, but the fourth, the perpetrator of the original sin, was unknown. A name so painful that it had been scored through. A black scar where once the truth had been spelled out. Reverend Soulsby's role had been clear, but now, he needed to fill in the blank – and for what he had done, he would have to suffer.

Entrapping him had been easy. He'd readily agreed to a meeting on a false promise. It was all timed perfectly. The rehearsal for the nativity play had finished, and the participants were quick to leave, eager to get home to their warm, centrally heated homes. They hurried out the church door and away through the graveyard. Wrapped up against the weather in scarves, hats and gloves, they focused on the steam their breath made in the cold night air, not the person waiting in the darkness.

Like All Saints, the Church of St Luke was bedecked in Christmas falsehoods. At the front, to one side, painted animals cut out from wooden board stood around a crib, in which a doll wrapped in a white cloth was lying.

'We've just had a dress rehearsal for the nativity,' Soulsby had cheerfully said, unaware that they'd been watching and waiting. 'I'll go and get changed.' His eyes smiled below the expanse of his brow and balding head, faint dimples appearing at the corners of his mouth.

'No. Stay in your shepherd's smock.'

Cold. Commanding. The change in voice tone made the vicar stop and look quizzically at them. The smile slipping.

The pathetic creature had no idea of what was coming. He glanced briefly at the bag and then back to their face. A face he trusted. A face he knew.

'How can I help you?' he'd asked.

'Sit down.'

His eyebrows raised, but he was trained not to show emotion. To serve and to be tolerant and pious. Had he been trained for what he'd done all those years ago?

Once the vicar was seated, they began.

'Forty years ago, when you were a curate, the then Bishop Warriner asked you to do something.'

They watched Soulsby's face closely. How much had that act played on his mind and conscience over the years? The speed with which he recognised what was being talked about would tell them that.

They waited. There it was. A quick glance away and a twitch of the corner of his lying mouth.

'He asked me to do lots of things. Forty years is a long time ago. You might need to be a little more specific.' His voice had taken on an overly cheerful tone, as though it could somehow derail their line of questioning.

'This was something immoral. Something you should never have done. Against the principles of the Church. Against decent human morality.'

There was no doubt that he knew exactly what they were talking about. He'd started to rub his hands together and then up and down his thighs, wiping the sweat from his palms. His top lip became moist despite the cold night.

Had he really thought it would go unmentioned? Unpunished?

'Look, I do apologise, but this is our busiest time of the year and I really don't know what you are referring to.' He made as if he was going to get up and go.

'I want to know a name. The name of the perpetrator. I know what part you played. I know what part the bishop played. But who were you protecting?'

'Really, I've no idea what you are talking about. Perhaps we can reconvene with this—' He didn't finish his sentence because his jaw dropped open at the sight of his questioner taking latex gloves and pulling them onto their hands.

The penny dropped.

Then, so did the vicar.

A swift blow to his head as he'd tried to get away left him sprawled face first on the hard stone floor. Soulsby let out a grunt and blood oozed from his mouth, where a tooth had pierced through his lip. A small gash marred his shiny bald head. A red welt of split pink skin.

His attacker worked quickly. Taking the plastic ties from a bag in their pocket and pulling them tight around Soulsby's wrists so that his arms were round the back of his body.

The church was a smorgasbord of DNA evidence. They weren't worried about that: it would be going up in flames shortly. But they needed to ensure that Soulsby's body didn't carry anything incriminatory. As before, anything that was used had been meticulously cleaned prior to coming, and then placed in a sealed bag. Once everything was done, they also had a bottle of bleach to ensure no traces of their involvement could be detected. They knew how these things worked.

While the vicar was out cold, they'd closed and locked the church doors. It was unlikely that anyone would be out so late on a night like tonight, but they couldn't take any chances. Reverend Soulsby was groaning awake by the time they were finished.

Using a foot, they rolled him over so that he was lying on his back. Blood seeped down his chin and onto the white dog collar around his neck.

'Why? I can help you. We can sort this out,' he stuttered. 'We can forget this ever happened.'

'You *can* help me. I need the name.'

'I don't know. The bishop never told me who. He just gave me the instruction.'

'Well, I know that you are more than capable of lying and so I've brought along a little aide-memoire.'

A short whip, studded with razor blades, was pulled from the bag.

'I believe it's customary for weak clergy to punish themselves and reaffirm their devotion by flogging or self-flagellation.'

A smile played on their lips as the Reverend Soulsby's eyes grew wider and fear turned to panic.

'Don't worry, I'll help you out. Wouldn't expect you to have to do it all yourself. But first, we're just going to double-check you didn't text anyone about our little meeting, or add it to one of those pesky online calendars. It wouldn't do for me to leave a calling card.'

The attacker fished the vicar's phone from his pocket, enjoying every moment of his distress. They pointed the screen at his face to enable access, and then they double-checked everything was in order. Finally, they could begin the process of retribution. It had been a long time coming.

The night was a long and painful one for Reverend Soulsby. As his church burned, he was able to watch, hidden from the emergency services who swarmed, trying to save the ancient place of worship while its vicar slowly suffered. By the time dawn showed its new face, he was finally at peace. The agony with which he'd gone to meet his God had been acute.

His killer was satisfied that he had, for once, told the truth. Reverend Soulsby had not known who the other was that had started the terrible chain of events. It was time to move on to the next name. The next victim.

5

DECEMBER 18TH

Morning arrived with a shrill beep from Harrison's alarm and slivers of fuchsia light squeezing through the gaps in the blinds. He felt sluggish and slightly off kilter. Tiny flashes of nightmares, vivid and violent, came to him. He'd been having disturbed sleep for a week now. He knew the trigger. You didn't need to be a psychologist to work that one out.

Finding out the truth about who his so-called father was, and coming face-to-face with his arch nemesis, Desmond Manning, were bad enough. Now he also had to deal with the reason why his mother had been killed, and that somebody in the police must have been at least partially responsible. Those were just his personal traumas. The day job wasn't exactly the stuff of picture book happy dreams, either.

Harrison knew he didn't have time to dwell on any of that now. There were people depending on him. He engaged his muscles and threw back the duvet. The small amount of dawn light coming into his room had already told him the sunrise was pretty spectacular and so he crossed to the window and pulled up the blind.

He felt an instant wave of awe, perspective, and relaxation. The sky was painted a stunning red, pink, and orange. Nature's colour palette had outdone herself. The winter sun was creating the burning orange glow as it rose from the horizon, and that blended into the pinks and a vivid red. Purple seemed to streak across the strata, the result of cloud reflecting the light. He was reminded of the old shepherd's weather rhyme. *Red sky at night, shepherds' delight. Red sky in the morning, shepherds' warning.* The sky indicated that the forecasters were probably right. There would be snow arriving, and soon.

The snow would no doubt be welcomed by children as they prepared to finish school for the festive break, and probably some parents too, who would be able to use it as an excuse to work from home and switch off early for their family Christmas. But for Dr Harrison Lane, there was no prospect of a slow wind down towards Christmas. Detective Inspector Sebastian Bartholomew from the National Crime Agency had called him yesterday to ask if he could head to Suffolk where a killer was burning churches and had already killed a verger, with fears that others would soon become victims.

Yesterday had been Harrison's last official day as Head of the Metropolitan Police's Ritualistic Behavioural Crime unit. From Monday, he and his assistant, Ryan, would be running their unit under the NCA. His expertise in ritualistic and religious crime had quickly found a far wider calling than just London's geography. Shame that criminals didn't take a bit of time off for Christmas though. He sorely needed a bit of downtime.

Harrison reluctantly turned his back on the sunrise and

headed to the shower, stripping his muscular body of pyjamas and enjoying the refreshing water that rained down on his scalp and skin. By the time he'd returned to his bedroom, the pale winter sun had risen, bleaching the sky of colour. The new day had begun.

Harrison re-packed his away bag, making sure he included his gym kit. Then he took a walk around the flat to check everything was in order. The fridge was as empty as it had been when he'd arrived home last night. He and Ryan had got a takeaway at the office and as he didn't drink tea or coffee, he had no need for milk. Breakfast had been a dandelion, fennel, and ginger tea. He'd get something to eat when he picked up the hire car. He glanced longingly at his bike keys on the kitchen worktop. The weather forecast meant taking his Harley was not going to be an option. It was a shame, he'd miss the feeling of freedom he got from riding the motorbike.

With a sigh, he closed the front door and headed out.

'HARRISON. I hope we didn't keep you up.' Harrison's rather jaded-looking neighbour was manhandling a full black bin liner out of his own flat on the floor below, the bag clinked and clanked with each movement, giving away its empty bottle and can filled contents.

'No. All good,' Harrison replied.

'Actually, I'm glad I've caught you,' his neighbour continued just as Harrison was about to walk past. 'I wanted to let you know I've sold my flat. We're going to be moving out of London.'

'OK.'

'Getting married in the spring and the price of properties here is crazy. Sold ours for over one point two million. Nuts.

We're going to be able to buy a nice house within commutable distance, and with offices for both of us so we can work from home *and* have no mortgage. No brainer really.'

'That's good. I hope it goes well,' Harrison replied.

'Yeah. You too.' His neighbour smiled, beginning to realise that this was not going to be an in-depth conversation. 'Merry Christmas,' he added and raised a hand to Harrison before disappearing back into his flat for another bag of recycling.

Harrison still didn't get the total preoccupation with Christmas. They'd not celebrated it much when he'd been a child due to their alternative way of life, and as his mother had died when he was eighteen, he'd had no family since to make it an annual tradition. Besides, apart from the fact he was distinctly agnostic, it irritated him that the whole festival was based on deception, a fake birth date. The Bible didn't say that the twenty-fifth of December was when Jesus was born and there was plenty of evidence to suggest it couldn't have been the date. He liked to live his life based on facts and Christmas was irrefutably a man-made fabrication, which was now the primary fuel for a retail bonanza.

As Harrison walked to pick up the hire car, he thought there was a strong likelihood that whoever was causing the murder and mayhem in Suffolk might also agree with his view of Christmas. Question was, what had driven them to such extremes? Burning churches and killing was more than just a bit of Christmas cynicism.

He'd just signed the contract for the car and been handed the keys, ready to start his journey, when his phone rang. It was DI Bartholomew.

'Harrison, you en route to Suffolk?'

'Just on my way now.'

'There have been two churches burned down now. We've got a dead verger and a missing vicar. The prime minister is taking an interest. It's not far from his constituency and those churches were ancient. One of them had some rare round tower. It's all over the media. You know what it's like this time of year. There's so little news that anything they can get their hands on is going to make the front pages, let alone a crime with a Christmas theme.

'The local police are treating the verger's death as manslaughter. Apparently he lived across the road, called the fire brigade and decided to play the hero and put the fire out himself. Unfortunately, he just succeeded in making it worse and killing himself. They're concerned about the missing vicar. He was last seen at a nativity rehearsal and seemed fine.'

'They don't consider him a suspect?'

'They're not thinking that's likely at this stage. But I don't think they've got much to go on. They need your input ASAP before we're presented with another dead body.'

6

DECEMBER 18TH

Harrison had been sent the initial reports into the two church blazes, but he worked best when able to look at a fresh crime scene. He never wanted the initial investigator's report to bias his thinking prior to reviewing it himself. Once information was in your head, it was hard to dismiss it or separate it from your own fact-based opinions. Consequently, he didn't read the full reports, just the situational summaries.

The issue with the fires was that not being early to the crime scene meant he couldn't use his own observational skills to their best effect. Years of training from his stepfather, a member of the Shadow Wolves, the elite Native American trackers, ensured he saw things that other people did not. But by the time he reached the two crime scenes in Suffolk, there would have been teams of people trampling over the evidence. Firemen, medical first responders and then police forensics and investigators. He'd have to rely on the forensics team recording what had been there.

His priority was the most recent fire. That was the freshest – and a man had gone missing from it.

To get there, he had to endure nearly three hours of driving, a reminder that he'd made the right decision about his motorbike. The car was heated and enclosed. Out the windows, the fields that he zoomed past were covered in frost. It had been below freezing overnight and temperatures had still not picked up, particularly after he'd left the warmer confines of the city and headed out into rural England.

As the M11 shrunk to the A11 and A14, and then the A143, the flat, rural landscape of Suffolk settled in. Tree-lined roads. Huge brown fields with the occasional green of winter cabbage and sprouts. Squares patterned with the white dots of sheep, or the occasional horse in a brightly coloured rug. The cows were in for the winter, and only the hardiest of ponies were left to face the falling temperatures. The fields were interrupted by the rooftops of villages, or electricity pylons, but as part of East Anglia, the most fertile land in England, Suffolk was heavily rural.

The area at the epicentre of the church burning was a conglomerate of small villages situated in between the Norfolk border and the Suffolk coastline. The villages had spread like puddles of water into each other so that it was hard to tell where one ended and the other began, apart from the road signs and the focal point of each one: their churches.

The sat nav told Harrison to peel right off the main road and, within minutes, he found himself in a picture-postcard English village. Black and white Tudor houses, perfect in their irregularity, a traditional pub with a lawned garden, and a small duck pond in the centre. It was beautiful. Until you looked towards the far end of the village and the picture post-card became a blackened nightmare. The church's stone tower reached up to the heavens, a stark salute over its gutted innards. The graveyard was still populated by a spaghetti of fire engine hoses and bright fluorescent emergency crew.

Harrison pulled into the pub car park, which seemed to have become a de facto police parking lot already, and stopped to view the scene in front of him.

The church was stone, but anything built out of timber, including the roof supports and the internal fittings, had been mostly consumed by the fire. The whole village stank of the acrid, charred remains. Fire crews were still sifting through the interior of the church, ensuring everything was dampened down – and no doubt ensuring the vicar wasn't somewhere in the debris.

Across the road, a fire officer on an aerial ladder platform tended to a thatched cottage, the last in the village before the fields beyond. There were clearly concerns that sparks could have settled into the thatch, waiting to ignite. It wouldn't be long before they'd start the investigation into the cause of the fire.

In front of this scene of devastation was a small gaggle of media, TV crews, reporters, and photographers. As Harrison arrived, the focus of their lenses wasn't on the sorry state of St Luke's church, but on a tall blonde woman who was giving a statement. Harrison suspected, based on her clothing and the commanding way in which she was talking to the media, that he was looking at DCI Lynne Turner, the senior investigating officer on the case. She cut a formidable figure, probably just over six feet in height, standing above the heads of many of the surrounding media.

Harrison had been sent a couple of names as his liaison contacts. As the DCI was busy, he approached one of the uniformed officers who was manning the cordon around the site. 'Is Detective Sergeant Patrick Howard around?' Harrison asked the young officer.

'He's over there talking with the fire chief.' The officer nodded over to where a young Black man in a full forensic oversuit was talking to an older man in a black uniform and cap. Harrison nodded his thanks and walked over to the pair.

'There are still some areas we haven't been able to sift through yet. We're going to have to wait until it cools, and there's a danger of the roof collapsing in at the far end there.'

'Is there any chance of a body lying undiscovered still?'

Before the fire chief answered, he became aware of Harrison, who had come to stand a couple of feet away from them.

DS Howard turned and raised his eyebrows at the eavesdropper.

'Can I help? Are you with the media?'

Harrison put his hand out. 'Doctor Harrison Lane, National Crime Agency. I head up the Ritualistic Behavioural Crime unit.'

DS Howard's face animated into a big smile.

'Doctor Lane, a pleasure to meet you. The detective superintendent said you were coming. We're so glad you could help out. Give me one moment.' He turned back to the fire chief.

'I'll let you get on, Doug, but are we still looking for a body in there?'

'Very unlikely, but it's always possible.'

DS Howard let out a big sigh and nodded his head in thanks. 'OK, cheers.'

As he turned round to Harrison, the fire chief headed back to the job. He and his crew looked tired. Two major blazes in two nights had taken it out of them.

'Second church we've lost, but this time we've got a missing vicar, too,' DS Howard explained.

'Was the death of the verger accidental or are you treating it as murder?'

'At this stage, everything is still open. Indications are it was accidental. The verger called 999 and we think he went into the church to try to put out the fire. We've no idea about Reverend Soulsby. He was here at a nativity rehearsal and that's the last he was seen or heard from. My gut feeling is he's not in the church.'

DS Howard looked wistfully at the charred remains of St Luke's and rubbed his chin absentmindedly.

'Can I go inside the cordon? Take a look around?' Harrison asked.

'You won't be able to go into the church yet. It's still not safe. But you're welcome to go into the graveyard area. I'll get you a suit and overshoes.' The DS waved at a forensics officer, who was just shutting up the back of a van, and walked over.

Harrison was ready a few minutes later, covered from head to toe in the crime scene coveralls, which would protect any evidence left by their perpetrator. While most of the scene was already compromised, if he found something or strayed off the beaten track, then preserving the integrity of the evidence would be vital. Before he went in to take a look, DS Howard gave him the timeline of events.

'Fire crews were alerted at just before 9 p.m. Multiple phone calls from members of the public in the surrounding area. When they got here, the church was already well alight. Found the same clay doll outside the main doors as they'd found at All Saints. Any idea what that's about?'

'Not yet. I'll need to take a look.'

'And you are?' A strong, stern, female tone interrupted their conversation.

Harrison turned to find the woman who had been entertaining the press earlier was now standing behind them, her arms folded across her chest in a manner which was clearly challenging him as to what he was doing at her crime scene. She was not a woman many would argue with.

'Dr Harrison Lane. The National Crime Agency sent me,' he replied. He didn't offer his hand because he'd already donned the nitrile gloves to prevent contamination. He also didn't rise to the challenge.

'Are you it?'

'What do you mean?' Harrison retorted. He didn't like the mocking tone of her voice.

'Are you the extra resources that the boss asked for?'

'I've not been party to discussions, but I'm head of the Ritualistic Behavioural Crime unit with the NCA and they asked me to come here as this looks like a religiously motivated series of attacks that aren't linked to any known terrorist threat.'

The DCI hmphed.

'I believe my detective superintendent asked for a detective, not a psychologist. I don't hold much faith in the American methods of profiling. It's Hollywood sensationalism based on guesswork. I only rate solid police work in my investigations.'

'I can assure you, DCI, that I work purely on facts. There's no guesswork with anything that I suggest. I'm also not just a profiler, I am an expert in ritualistic and religious crime—'

'Really!' she sarcastically replied, cutting him short. She was clearly someone who didn't shy away from confrontation. A woman who used her height and fitness, along with her rank, to achieve dominance. These were tactics she would probably have learned to use from her childhood, when her height would have attracted the bullies.

Harrison was doing his best to not allow a flicker of the anger he was feeling to show on his face or in his body language. He made an effort to smile, but realised that he was clenching his fists by his side – he could feel the latex of the gloves tightening on the back of his hand. He wasn't intimidated, but had taken an immediate dislike to her personality and working style.

'I don't know what you're doing here. We need to be out there looking for Reverend Soulsby – I don't think he's in these smouldering ruins.' She said that as much to the DS as to Harrison.

'There are no leads so far, ma'am,' DS Howard replied in an apologetic tone. 'We have teams out making inquiries.'

Just then, one of the TV reporters walked over, microphone extended, camera crew in tow, ready for a quote.

'DCI Turner, is there any truth in the rumour that this is linked to paganism?'

Harrison watched the cold dead eyes of the DCI change to a sparkling smile as she turned round to greet the reporter.

Harrison and the DS took the interruption as their getaway opportunity. They quickly signed into the access record book for the crime scene and ducked under the tape, away from where the DCI was again lapping up her camera time.

'So, that's the DCI,' DS Howard muttered. 'Sorry about that. She's not usually quite so prickly. She was off sick with Covid when this started up and the detective superintendent was worried that we wouldn't have enough resources. She doesn't take too kindly to interference from outside.'

Harrison noted the information but said nothing.

'So, you know the timeline?' the DS continued. 'In all honesty, that's pretty much all we have. We don't know how he got in, if he'd surprised the vicar, none of it because there's no evidence yet. Although it's likely he used an accelerant to start the fire. That's the indications so far with All Saints.'

'No idea how he made his getaway?'

'We have a neighbour who heard a car shortly before they noticed the fire, so it's possible he left with the vicar by road. We're checking for any potential CCTV on routes through the village. There's a camera at a house on the main road out, so I'm hoping that's going to give us something. The vicar's car is still in the car park.'

'I'd like to take a walk around myself. Anyone else been through the graveyard besides fire crew and Forensics?'

'No. We've had the site locked down since we got here. Perimeter is this side from the graveyard and we have an officer on the other side of the field behind making sure nobody crosses in that way.'

'OK,' Harrison added and waited.

'Oh, OK. Right. I'll be over there.' He finally got the hint that Harrison wanted to be alone. 'Take my card, it's got my mobile number and contact details.'

Absolute concentration was critical for Harrison. He wasn't being rude; he just needed to ensure there were no distractions. He needed to get inside the head of the person who had done this. Work out what they might have done next.

If they had any hope of finding the vicar alive, then this was going to be it.

Totally focusing was a challenge in the midst of the activity in and around the church, and yet it was essential that Harrison did just that. He was aware of the emergency crews, the media, and the onlookers who had come out of their homes to look at the devastation to their church and the resulting investigation. They didn't need to watch TV or read a newspaper for drama. It was on their doorsteps.

Harrison stopped a moment and turned round to look at the various people who were gathered outside the cordon. It was a well-known fact that perpetrators often revisit their crime scenes, enjoying seeing the impact of their handiwork and feeling a sense of power that they could watch on while investigators struggled to work out what had happened and who was responsible. In this case, the dramatic nature of the crime and its visual impact made that an even more likely scenario.

At this stage, they didn't know if Reverend Soulsby had come to any harm. He could have been distraught about the fire and had some kind of breakdown. Or he could have set the fire himself. The only evidence that there was a second person involved was the witness saying they had heard another car. It wasn't much to go on, and could have been totally unconnected. But it clearly wasn't Reverend Soulsby – his car was still parked up. So where was he?

Besides the media, Harrison estimated there were around fifteen locals gathered, including another vicar. He looked at each one of their faces, their body language, searching for any signs that they were enjoying the spectacle, and he took a few photographs. Then he turned his back on them all and closed his eyes.

Harrison first placed his ear buds in and allowed Guns N' Roses, 'November Rain', to fill his ears and cancel out the chatter and sounds of the investigation. With the familiar guitar riffs, he was able to focus totally on his breathing and block out the world around him.

He felt each breath as he pulled it into his chest and abdomen. Heard its escape as he pushed it back out again. In and out, counting to four with each movement. In. One, two, three, four. Out. One, two, three, four. Repeat. Only when his mind had settled. Once he was aware of every muscle in his body, was he ready to start work.

The area around the church was already heavily trampled by the fire crews and sodden with the water from their hoses, but Harrison started there and looked for anything radiating out. A forensic sweep would have already been carried out for anything dropped that could incriminate or even indicate what had happened and by who, but objects weren't Harrison's main concern. He was on a manhunt.

The main entrance faced the village – a risky point of entry and exit, unless you were supposed to be there. The fire was reported in the early evening when it was perfectly feasible for people to have still been up and about and have noticed the perpetrator, especially if they had a reluctant vicar in tow. Unless, of course, it was the reverend himself who had done it, but his car was still on site.

Harrison walked around the full perimeter of the church, scanning the ground and looking for any signs of damage which couldn't be obviously attributed to the firefighters. Every step was a slosh or squelch on the sodden ground. It was impossible. Two crews had hauled hoses and other equipment around in a desperate bid to save the ancient building. Anything that had been there to see was obliterated.

There was only one other way to get into the church, and that was a side entrance which was tucked away from sight, and which would give someone more privacy if they wanted to come and go unseen. If their pyromaniac was smart, this would have been the most likely exit route.

Harrison scanned the area. Again, for the first few feet around the doorway, the ground was wet and trampled, but as he moved further away into the graveyard, the operational water damage grew less noticeable. At the time of the fire, the ground hadn't been frozen, but overnight temperatures had dropped, and they hadn't risen much. It was still solid underfoot. If someone had gone that way, there was a good chance their footprints might remain, even if someone else had stepped on them since.

His eyes searched, looking for indentations: the way the grass had been flattened, broken twigs, the crescent of a heel, a scuffed grave. He was almost beginning to think he'd find nothing when he picked up the trail. Two sets of footprints, one with shoes, one barefoot, heading out of the graveyard and through the gate that led into the field. Being careful not to tread on them, he left the church and set off on their trail, a knot of anticipation tightening in his belly.

7

DECEMBER 18TH

'What the hell is that bloody idiot doing?'

The DCI's razor-sharp bark made DS Patrick Howard jump. He spun round to look at the knitted brows of his boss. Her eyes burned with the anger which creased her face in pent up frustration.

'Why the hell have you let him loose in our crime scene?' She moved her glare from the DS to the disappearing back of Harrison Lane.

'Ma'am. He's fully suited up. He asked to look around on his own.'

'So why's he heading out into a field of bloody sheep? I told you, we're wasting our time. We need to be focusing all our resources on where Reverend Soulsby might be. That means contacting all his known associates and running background checks to see if he or anyone else has been acting strangely lately. Stop babysitting that bloody idiot and get back to the office.'

'I was going to speak to Reverend Galloway. He's arrived to see if he can offer any assistance.'

'Well, get on with it then.'

DS HOWARD WATCHED his boss as she stropped off to talk to the mayor, Lucas Fry, who had arrived to offer help and join the collective sighing and headshaking of his community. He figured her mood was because she was going to be under pressure to get this case solved. It was Christmas, the worst possible time for someone to be burning down historic churches, and she looked tired already. Her obsessive control mentality meant she'd probably come back from Covid sick leave too early. They'd had a few other colleagues who had taken weeks to fully get their energy levels back up to speed again. The tiredness was clearly making her even more crotchety than usual.

He sighed and headed over to Reverend Galloway, who was comforting an elderly woman.

'The Bible tells us that the church is not a building but a gathering of believers who come together to worship. Our community and our faith will survive this destruction. History has proven that. All our churches are open to everyone. If you are unable to get transport, we'll make arrangements for you to come to St. Peter's. We will get through this together.'

'Thank you, vicar,' the lady replied faintly, but the tears remained in her milky eyes as she looked at the remains of the church she'd been christened and married in, and had expected to bid farewell from.

Reverend Galloway smiled reassuringly at the woman. He had a kind face which was welcoming and non-judgemental. He looked like a benign accountant in a dog collar. Blessed with a full head of hair, the silver flecks framed his face, and served to give him authority.

Patrick had hovered for a few moments, allowing the vicar to finish talking to the woman and for her to wander off, before he stepped forward and introduced himself.

'How long have you known Reverend Soulsby?' he asked.

'Oh, a long time. About forty years. We trained together. We've been lucky in this diocese, there has been very limited turnover and our congregations have held up. All of us are happy within our communities. The late Bishop Warriner valued that continuity. I doubt the current bishop will hold the same view going forward. Especially now.'

'Had Reverend Soulsby been acting any differently lately? Showing any signs of being worried about something?'

'No. Absolutely not. He loves this time of year. It's busy. Tiring. But he's a frustrated thespian at heart and the nativity play is the highlight of the season for him.'

'And you have no idea of anyone who might be behind these fires? Someone who might bear a grudge? You've not received any warnings yourself?'

Reverend Galloway shook his head vigorously and frowned some more. 'This is all out of the blue. I've absolutely no idea.'

DS Howard was about to continue when his mobile phone rang. It was a number he didn't recognise. He answered anyway.

'It's Harrison Lane. I've found him.'

8

DECEMBER 18TH

The two tracks of footprints were an easy trail for Harrison to follow. Joe had taught him to see the slightest disturbances on the ground or in the surrounding vegetation. He also knew he wasn't looking at emergency service personnel tracks or even a parishioner taking a country stroll. Nobody in their right mind would be walking outside in this cold weather without shoes. Harrison feared the worst.

The first field was empty, and on the far side he could see a squad car parked at the gate. The police knew from experience that the photographers, TV crews, and even the general public always wanted to get closer than they were allowed and this would have been a good back door for them. It was a necessary precaution to protect the crime scene. It was also a good route for the perpetrator to lead Reverend Soulsby away without being seen. They could have parked up in the same spot where the police car now was and driven away through the quiet country roads, avoiding the village and any potential CCTV.

The footprints didn't, however, head to the gate.

Around halfway across the field, Harrison saw heavier indentations and a handprint. Whoever was barefoot had fallen down here, to their knees by the looks of it, and placed their hands on the ground to break their fall. The gait of the barefoot person had already been ragged, as though they were struggling to walk. At times, the companion wearing shoes must have helped them because their imprints occasionally dug deeper into the soil, as though extra weight had borne down on them.

Harrison carried on following the trail to a small gate, which led into another field. He paused. If he opened the gate, he could potentially smudge any finger prints – the pair of tracks showed they'd stopped and opened the gate before progressing. He would have to go over it; he had his gloves on so he wasn't worried about contamination.

Before he jumped over, Harrison studied the ground on the other side, ensuring that he didn't obliterate the tracks. He also scanned across the field beyond, which was full of sheep. Nothing obvious, apart from there was another gate leading to the road. Perhaps that was where they'd parked up.

As he climbed over, the extra height gave Harrison a clearer view across the field and over the backs of its woolly inhabitants. There was a cluster of them around what looked like some hay near to the roadside gate, probably deposited there by the farmer that morning. Further over to the left, in the far corner, there was another cluster of sheep and several crows, flapping and landing among them. Something seemed different about this grouping. Harrison looked down at the tracks. They led directly to that far corner.

As Harrison walked diagonally across the field, the sheep looked up at him nervously, moving out of the way of the big man who had invaded their peaceful corner of the world. His stomach knotted. He wasn't sure what he was about to come across, but he didn't think it was going to be good. The second he could confirm anything, he would have to stop and make a phone call.

Harrison continued to looked carefully at the tracks, more to ensure that he wasn't trampling on them than anything else; it was obvious where they led. The only change was that the barefoot person's walking had grown increasingly erratic. As they'd travelled across this field, they'd fallen down several times. There was no blood, no obvious signs that the person was injured, but perhaps being out in the cold had been enough to sap their energy.

Halfway across the field, Harrison realised why the gathering of sheep had looked strange. They weren't real. They seemed to be wooden or cardboard cut-out sheep.

He stopped for a moment and looked back towards the roadside gate. It was barely visible. The field's camber meant that the farmer could have come and fed the sheep, watered them, even counted them, and not seen what was in that far corner.

Harrison's breathing had become more shallow. He'd seen many crime scenes and murder victims, but being confronted with the raw depravity of humanity was always extremely unpleasant. He suspected he was about to have to face it again. The presence of the crows was another warning. They were cawing and flapping. Arguing about something. Flying up and then coming back down again in the same area. He quickened his pace.

By the time he was three-quarters of the way across the field, he could see a brown mound on the ground next to the fake sheep, with crows on top of it.

A few more feet and Harrison realised what he was looking at.

In front of him, kneeling and slumped forward, was the body of a man. Barefoot and wearing what looked like a long brown smock shirt. The man's back was covered in bloody welts and the crows were pecking at the flesh through the slashed cloth.

He ran the rest of the way, a sickening in his stomach. The man could still be alive, although in Harrison's heart, he knew that was highly unlikely. He also ran to scare away the crows. Dead or not, the man deserved respect.

As he reached the body, he saw the full extent of the bloody injuries on the man's back. Carefully, Harrison reached for his neck and felt for a pulse. It took him seconds to realise there would be none: his body was cold and rigid. Life had left his corpse many hours before.

Harrison retreated a few feet and took in the scene in front of him. There were three or four wooden sheep next to what he assumed to be Reverend Soulsby. He was still wearing what looked likely to be his nativity costume. Even if the injuries to his back hadn't killed him, lying out here in the freezing cold field overnight in just the thin smock probably would have.

His arms had been pulled behind his body and secured with a black plastic zip tie. His feet were, as Harrison would have expected, caked in mud and an unhealthy colour of death and cold. Harrison couldn't see his face in detail because he'd slumped forward, but there was some form of gag around his mouth and head, and blood had seeped out. It was unlikely to be as a result of decomposition yet and so Harrison assumed that some kind of injury had taken place to his mouth.

Harrison sighed and pulled his phone from his pocket to dial DS Patrick Howard.

Once he had shared his news, he stood vigil over the body. He wanted to check where the shoed feet had gone after this point, but that would have to wait. The crows lined the trees all around him, cawing and rasping. Angry that they had been interrupted. Waiting impatiently for their chance to come back down and finish their lunch. He was going to make absolutely sure that didn't happen.

Somewhere in the back of his mind, he remembered that a group of crows was called a murder. The irony didn't escape him. It was very obvious that Reverend Soulsby's death was definitely not through natural causes. Harrison shivered, but not from the cold. He stood in the strange field, with crows all around, a slate grey sky pressing down on him and only sheep to bear witness to the sorry remains of a human life he shared it with.

It sparked a childhood memory that brought on a heavy sadness and a tightening in his chest as he relived the feeling of helplessness. As a child in the Arizona desert, he knew that the circling of the turkey vultures would always give away the location of an injured or dying creature. He'd hated their black feathers and bald red heads, which looked like they'd just been ripping away at bloody flesh.

They'd had a pet dog in those days. A mongrel Harrison called Bob. He had adopted them. Just turned up on their doorstep one day hungry and thirsty. He'd sat down next to Harrison and put his head on his lap. The bond was instant.

Harrison loved that dog for two years, until one day Bob didn't come back from his wandering. Harrison had gone looking for him, trying to use the tracking skills his stepfather had taught him. Calling his name until his voice was hoarse and his legs exhausted. As the sky darkened and he turned back for home, he'd seen them. Turkey vultures circling a few hundred yards away.

By the time Harrison reached Bob, the vultures were tearing at his carcass. He'd run at them screaming, flapping his arms to scare them off, but they were big and he was only young. They'd hopped a short way away, but they didn't go far, watching him with their beady eyes, wondering if he was up to the fight, or if he might be the next meal.

Harrison had picked up Bob's bloody body and started carrying it home. Through two long miles he'd walked along the dusty dirt track road, accompanied every step of the way by the threatening black shadows of the vultures above him. Occasionally, one would land just ahead of him in a tree and watch every step he took as he went past. Waiting for him to trip. To show any sign of weakness.

Most of the way home, he'd sobbed into the fur of his friend. Devastated that he'd not been able to protect him from the sickening attack.

Later, Joe had come to him and explained that Bob must have been hit by a car. He had a big gash on his head and had probably died instantly. He also told him that the vultures were a necessary part of life. Clearing up after death. Harrison understood the practicalities, but it had done little to drive away the nightmare of the whole experience and his sense of loss.

Harrison stood sentinel over the body of Reverend Soulsby. The crows couldn't hurt him, but if they were to have the best chance of getting justice for him, then they needed to keep the body and crime scene as forensically intact as possible. His other motivation was the thought of the man's family and friends who would be devastated enough by his loss and method of departure, without the knowledge that carrion had been feasting on his remains.

Harrison didn't have to wait too long before DS Howard came bounding across the field with forensics and DCI Turner in pursuit. He'd given them strict guidance: to avoid opening the gate, be careful of the tracks and not park any vehicles in the gateway in case they could find car tyre imprints from their killer.

'Shit,' was the DS's professional opinion as he approached Harrison. He crouched down a few feet away, peering at the face of their corpse. 'Definitely looks like the Reverend Soulsby. What the hell's going on with the sheep?' DS Patrick Howard looked from the painted wooden cut-out sheep to Harrison. The faces of the sheep caricatures were cute and smiley, totally incongruous in their current position.

'My guess is the reverend is in his nativity costume and the sheep would have been part of the set.'

'How the hell did they get all the way out here?'

'From the tracks, I'd say he carried them.'

'Poor bugger. Looks like he's been stabbed multiple times in the back.'

By now, the lead forensics' officer had come up alongside them. A big man in his fifties with a face that had seen it all and a lot more.

'That doesn't look like stab wounds. I'd say it's more like slashes. And were the birds attacking him?' he puffed.

Harrison nodded.

'Right. We need to get this lot covered ASAP.' He barked into a radio at his team, calling various personnel to check out the gateways for tyre tracks and fingerprints, take casts of the footprints, and put a tent over the remains of Reverend Soulsby.

'How did you find him?' The sharp tone of DCI Lynne Turner made Harrison and DS Howard turn round. She stood, now wearing the full forensics garb over her smart suit, staring at the mound of human flesh that had once been the vicar of St Luke's.

'I followed their tracks,' Harrison replied. 'From the graveyard, across the first field and into here. He was barefoot, so stood out a mile.'

She said nothing. No thank you or well done. Nothing.

'I don't want this getting back to the media. They already think something's up after we all rushed off. We need to keep this under wraps until we've confirmed identity and spoken to his wife. That clear? Get some extra uniforms to make sure no one comes near this field.'

'Yes, ma'am,' DS Howard replied.

Harrison didn't grace her orders with a reply. Instead, content that the victim was now being well guarded, he started to follow the shoe tracks away from the crime scene and towards the roadside gate.

'Where's he going now?' He heard the DCI say in the distance to DS Howard.

Once Harrison reached the gate, the tracks were obliterated by hundreds of sheep hoof imprints and the occasional large wellington print. Harrison turned to look back up the field. The only thing visible were the shoulders and heads of the forensics officers and DCI Turner. DS Howard was on his way down the field like a panicked babysitter chasing an errant child.

Harrison climbed the gate to look the other side. Thick wide tyre tracks had gone over the top of those before it. The farm vehicle, which had brought the hay for the sheep, had also brought water with it and that had run into the ground, thawing the mud. They might salvage something, but it was going to be a long shot.

He stopped for a few moments, lost in thought, before DS Howard caught up with him. Whoever had done this to

Reverend Soulsby had planned everything with precision. Question was whether he was going to be the only victim? Was the first fire just a practice and this one the real thing, or was this just the start of something that was going to get far worse? Harrison had the sickening feeling it was the latter.

9

———————

DECEMBER 18TH

Harrison stayed at the crime scene long enough to hear the attending pathologist's initial observations. They would be unpleasant reading for his family, but gave Harrison some indications as to the killer's state of mind.

Afterwards, DS Patrick Howard suggested they head back to the incident room so that he could familiarise himself with the rest of the evidence they'd found so far. In truth, Harrison needed the break. The long drive, the cold, tracking, and then being confronted with Reverend Soulsby's body were enough to dent anyone's energy and concentration.

Visiting the crime scene that morning had more than served its purpose. Now he needed to look at the clay dolls that had been left at both fires, and start to pull together some kind of theory as to what the pyromaniac killer was trying to achieve. There was nothing more for him to do here. It was over to Forensics and the pathologist to do their jobs.

'There's a great little cafe next door to the station,' DS

Howard said to Harrison as they walked back to their cars. 'I'm getting a bacon butty and a coffee. Fancy anything?'

DS Howard had taken off his forensic overalls, and Harrison could see the man liked to dress smartly. His suit was well fitted, and the tie looked silk.

'A bacon sandwich would be good. Thank you.' Harrison replied, suddenly remembering he'd not stopped for that breakfast he'd promised himself. No wonder he was starting to flag. The high sugar and carb content of his Chinese take-away last night would have well and truly worn off and his body was in need of refuelling.

'Ketchup?' DS Howard asked. 'Gotta have a bit of ketchup, right?'

He nodded, and DS Howard grinned. Harrison liked the DS already – and distinctly *disliked* his boss. It was going to be an interesting few days working with them both.

THE INCIDENT ROOM was a commandeered section of a small regional police station. It was cramped, but secure and connected to all they needed. The walls were painted in a sickly lime colour, a throwback to interior decor fashion that had long been forgotten. Either that or it had just been a cheap end-of-line purchase when budgets were running low.

The room looked out over the main street of the neighbouring village to where Harrison had spent his morning. A vanload of mobile incident room equipment had been delivered and most of it was in the process of being distributed around the room onto the various rickety old desks which looked like they'd been pulled out of a 1980s storage area.

The chairs were old and stained with countless caffeine spillages over the years. Harrison's chair had obviously run out of gas in its pneumatic height adjustment system and consequently he sat with his knees higher than his hips, like he had somehow found himself in a scene from *Alice in Wonderland*, towering tall after eating the cake that made you grow.

He swapped the chair over. Perhaps somebody who wasn't six foot two might make better use of it. Once he'd managed to adjust the new chair so he was comfortable, he took his leather jacket off and slung it over the back in the hope of claiming it as his own for at least today. The room was already filling up with technical and admin staff.

By the time Harrison had logged onto the computer system, DS Howard was back with a brown paper bag that left an aroma of bacon in its wake. It was good to replace the acrid smoke particles in their nostrils with something far more palatable. Even better once the food hit their stomachs.

'So what do you reckon was going on with that nativity scene in the field?' he asked Harrison. 'Someone got something against Christmas or sheep?' He had taken his suit jacket off and placed it over the back of a chair before eating his roll carefully. A serviette was tucked into his shirt collar, with another on his lap and a third wrapped around the bacon roll to ensure no grease or ketchup was let loose on his clothes.

'I'm not sure yet. I need to see more before I can form a full opinion,' Harrison replied, but didn't bother with answering the obvious. The sheep were clearly not the target.

'Oh yeah, you wanted to see those clay dolls. They've both gone to the lab for testing, but we've got loads of photos on the system.'

He stood up and crossed to Harrison's desk, where he made several clicks of his mouse and took him through to a folder of images. He pulled one up big on the screen and stepped back.

Staring at Harrison was a primitive clay figure.

'Looks like a figurine of a woman or something. But she seems to be wearing a helmet and carrying a shield. Can't be Mary, so who is it?'

Harrison shook his head. 'Not Mary, no. That doesn't fit with what they're doing. It could be some kind of offering.'

'Offering? You mean like a cult or pagan worshippers?'

'I think the date of these fires is significant. I'll need to check something, but it's not Christian.' Something was in the back of Harrison's mind, but he couldn't quite place it.

The DS had finally finished his bacon roll and started removing his protective paper napkin armour. 'It looks like the stuff you make garden pots out of,' he suggested.

'Terracotta.'

'Yeah, like those Chinese warriors. Do you think it could be Chinese?'

Harrison shook his head.

'I don't get why? What has this to do with burning a church and killing a vicar?'

Harrison was starting to form some hypotheses, but he needed to gather more information first. He'd learned from experience that it was better to keep tight-lipped and only share any theories once he was completely confident about what he was saying. His encounters with DCI Turner under-lined the necessity of that tactic.

'It's clearly highly symbolic to the killer. They're giving us a clue about their motivation and state of mind.'

DS Howard shook his head at the image in defeat. 'I'd better talk to the guys who are looking through the CCTV, to see if they've managed to spot anything. The DCI will be back soon and she'll want a briefing with the team.'

Harrison got the impression this was a warning about her

expectations, as much as it was the DS sharing his next steps. He wouldn't be rushed by anyone.

Harrison's main question now was what had been the motive at the first church? Reverend Soulsby wasn't an accidental victim; his death had clearly been premeditated given the way it had been staged. The kneeling position also gave the impression of a man atoning for a sin, begging for his life and forgiveness.

If the vicar was the reason for the second church attack, what was the first? They'd had no reports of anyone missing and everyone was pretty certain that the verger had died accidentally trying to put out the fire. Or maybe that was what the killer had wanted them to think.

He looked again at the images of the clay dolls. Right now there were still far more questions than facts.

Harrison glanced at the time. The day was already well over halfway done. He needed help getting moving with the background research. Something to put meat on the bones he'd managed to gather. It was time to get his assistant, Ryan, on the case.

10

———

DECEMBER 18TH

Ryan Chapman was staring out of his flat window at the busy street below. One side of his flat was quiet, overlooking the residential street where the entrance to the building was located. And then there was this side. Through the window, he could see Christmas present panic buying unfolding in full frenzy, helped by a sprinkling of sales in some shops. The scene in front of him seemed to contradict the news that the economic downturn had kept the shoppers away from the high street and caused budgets to be tightened. But there was nothing like an impending deadline and fear of disappointed faces on Christmas Day to encourage people to spend more than they could really afford and worry about it later.

Happy families around the tree with stockings bulging with presents weren't the memories now flooding back in Ryan's head. The years of his childhood had started with promise. A tree. Some gifts. But by Christmas lunch, the arguments between his mother and father would have started and the likelihood of her not having a bruise or split lip in time for eating it would have been slim. He'd retreat to his room and focus on his computer, rarely coming out unless he'd been commanded to, or occasionally to protect his mother when the arguments got too heated.

At some point over the years, his mother started to drink. This usually meant the arguments were even worse because the alcohol lessened her common sense survival instincts and she argued back. Once the booze no longer worked to dull the pain, she'd turned to drugs. During her decline, his dad had left them to it.

She hadn't been a bad mother. Even during her worst days, she had still done her best to care for him. What made him sad was that her love for him hadn't been enough to give her the strength she needed to stop her downward spiral, and he had been too young to help her.

The last Christmas they had spent together, she'd made a big effort to buy him gifts and put up some decorations to celebrate. Unfortunately, by Christmas morning, she'd sold the whole lot in order to get her next hit and Ryan had eaten baked beans for his lunch that year, accompanied by her sobbing apologies. Soon after, he'd started helping the dealer who supplied his mother – not because he wanted to, but because if he didn't, then he'd have had nothing to eat.

His mum was eventually arrested one time too many for shoplifting and sent to prison. He found himself on his own at fifteen and facing the care system. Ryan had run. Run straight into the arms of the drugs gang, who knew just how valuable his technology talents could be and who duly enrolled him onto their payroll.

His agoraphobia had gotten worse over the years, and it meant he was totally isolated from anyone who could have possibly helped him. Those years as he approached adulthood were ones he wished he could erase from his memory and conscience. He shuddered to think about where he'd be now without Harrison's intervention. Who he could have hurt. Every key stroke, every mouse click he did as Harrison's assistant, was atonement. It was also grateful thanks to the man himself.

The consequence of his upbringing and his fear of busy open spaces meant Ryan had never been Christmas shopping. He couldn't see the faces of the shoppers below him, but he longed for the pleasure that came from giving somebody a gift. This year he had several people to buy presents for, and although it was all done online, he'd enjoyed it. DS Jack Salter had invited them round for Christmas Day with his wife, Marie, and their son, Daniel. Harrison and Dr Tanya Jones would also be going.

Ryan had spent hours trawling the internet for the right presents for each of them, and as they came through the post to his front door, they'd brought smiles to his face at the thought of the pleasure they would bring. But it was the one gift which now sat, wrapped and alone on the table beside him, which had taken up most of his thoughts.

His mother had been released from prison and after going through the drugs rehab course while in there, had assured him she was clean. The letter from her had arrived a few weeks ago at his old flat. He'd still not replied. The battle between resentment and love raged in his heart and the fear of being hurt all over again prevented him from moving forward.

Ryan looked from the window to the handwritten letter. Since he'd come out of hiding from the authorities, he'd always known that it would be possible that one day she might get in contact with him. On the ten pages of blue notepaper beside him, she had poured her heart out. Begging his forgiveness and promising that she had changed. Telling him just how much she loved him and that she'd never stopped thinking and worrying about him. He knew she wasn't lying.

When Harrison had found him and helped him, he'd told Ryan how his social services file was filled with request after request from his mother to find out where he was and to get in contact. She hadn't believed the authorities that he'd gone on the run. She thought they were hiding him from her. Harrison had given Ryan a second chance at life, but he wasn't sure if he was ready to give his mother hers.

The sound of his mobile phone ringing broke Ryan from his internal debate. His boss's name flashed up on the screen. Time to get to work. He turned his back on the letter and the gift, and crossed to his desk.

Ryan's desk area took up a good chunk of his living space. He never had visitors around, so he didn't need more than just one small sofa, and he didn't care whether the place was tidy. His penchant for junk food and snacks was as evident here as it had been on his desk in their basement office at Scotland Yard. He was like a mouse, nest building with the empty wrappers, making himself feel safe and at home.

'How's it going, boss?' he asked as he answered the call.

'We've got a murdered vicar from last night's fire, and what looks like probably accidental death with a verger from the first one – but we can't rule out murder, so need to keep an open mind on that for now.'

'Not exactly full of Christmas spirit in Suffolk, are they?'

'No.'

Harrison never was very good at the subtleties of communications. Humour and banter were alien languages to him.

'I need you to dig up everything you can on the two churches, St Luke's and All Saints, plus the dead pair,' Harrison continued. 'Are they connected? Any scandals or accusations over the years? This has the smack of revenge or justice to me, but I've little to go on yet. The DCI in charge is... Well, let's just say I think she's strong-minded. I have a feeling she's not going to be keen to listen to my views, so I might need some additional support.'

'No problem. Just let me know what you need.'

'Everything else OK your end?'

'Yeah, yeah. National Crime Agency hasn't sent anything else through yet. We had a couple of leftover requests from the Met, but they were straightforward. I can give this my full attention.' Ryan's subconscious mind made him glance over at the gift and letter on the table. He pulled his eyes away quickly.

'Thanks.'

With that, Harrison was gone.

Ryan stretched his arms out in front of him and interlaced his hands, clicking his fingers and wrists. He woke up his computer screen feeling both a sense of peace and excitement. This was what he lived for. Time to get to work.

11

DECEMBER 18TH

It wasn't just her height that ensured the room changed with her presence. When DCI Lynne Turner swept into the incident room, it was as though a ripple of anxiety followed in her wake. The level of activity seemed to step up a gear, but Harrison doubted it was productive activity, doubted that the team were achieving more and instead were just trying harder to look like they were doing more.

'Briefing in fifteen minutes. I want updates from you all,' she barked at the room, before sitting down at a large desk at the front. She barely glanced at Harrison.

He watched as everyone prepared for the briefing and wondered if she'd ever had any bullying complaints against her. Bullies were his pet hate – that, and all those who used peoples' beliefs and weaknesses to do harm.

Harrison used the fifteen minutes to continue looking through the witness statements taken by officers after both of the fires. They were, unfortunately, pretty unilluminating. Nobody had seen anything until the fires were lit or noticed anyone hanging around or acting strangely beforehand.

There'd been no threats received and no claims of responsibility from groups.

Yet there was a clear message in the way that Reverend Soulsby had been killed. The killer had gone to a lot of trouble to plan and carry out their murder.

Once the allotted time span was up, DCI turner stood to her full height and surveyed the room. It fell silent. Harrison was reminded of another female officer, DCI Sandra Barker, who could also make a room fall silent – only she did it through respect, not fear.

'We have two dead members of the clergy and two historic buildings destroyed. I don't need to tell you that this is receiving national attention because you can look out the window and see the TV crews and media camped outside. This should not be happening on our patch. We are losing lives and we're losing our heritage. I want results and fast.'

The DCI turned to the incident board behind her. 'We know that someone purposely set a fire at All Saints' church two nights ago. What we don't have is a motive. Justin Black, the verger who lived across the road, saw the fire and it looks like he ran in to try to put it out single-handedly. The coroner's report said there were no other injuries. He appears to have died of smoke asphyxiation and burns. An empty fire extinguisher was found next to his body. Last night, however, was a different matter. Again, our perp set fire to a church, this time St Luke's, but they didn't stop there. Reverend Martin Soulsby's body was found in an adjoining field. He'd been tortured.'

The DCI gave no recognition to Harrison for the find, but that didn't bother him.

'The vicar is on his way to the morgue now and we've asked for an urgent autopsy. Initial indications are that he was flogged with a sharp object and razor blades were put inside his mouth before he was gagged. He was found wearing only a thin shepherd's smock, which he'd worn earlier that evening at a dress rehearsal for the nativity play. Cause of death could have been hypothermia, shock, or blood loss. Around him were the wooden sheep from the play. Again, no obvious motive. Why burn the church? Why target Reverend Soulsby?'

She paused for dramatic effect and scanned the room. Harrison had never heard such a quiet briefing audience before.

'I need answers. Updates. DS Howard.'

'Ma'am.' Patrick jumped up to attention. 'We've gone through all the CCTV around All Saints, and there's nothing. Whoever did this knew which way to approach the area and to make their getaway. They must have used the side entrance because there were cameras on the main doors. So far, we've only located two potential CCTV opportunities in the village around St Luke's and we're on them, but it appears that the killer made his escape through the second field and onto Woolerton Lane, so there's unlikely to be any witnesses or cameras.'

The DS watched his boss's reaction closely before he continued.

'Getting any kind of evidence from the church buildings is going to be highly unlikely due to fire damage, but an accelerant was used at both sites and we should get a detailed report on that today. Our best possibility is going to be Reverend Soulsby himself – if there's third-party DNA or anything that could give us a clue as to who he was with just prior to his death.'

'What about potential motives and suspects?' She pushed him.

'Indications are that they knew the area well and that

these crimes were pre-planned. There were no reports of any threats against the vicar, or anyone who had been hanging around or causing trouble.'

'So where are we looking?'

'A small group of travellers has camped up at the cross-roads on the road to Lowestoft,' an officer spoke up to Harrison's right.

He sighed. He'd seen this before, where a lack of any kind of motive or suspect led to a witch hunt against any groups who weren't considered mainstream.

'There's also that group of new age hippies, druids in the forest a mile or so out of St Mary's. That's only about three miles from St Luke's and about the same distance to All Saints.' Another detective in front spoke now. 'They'd been quite vocal against the Church's recent campaign to encourage people to come to services, especially around Christmas.'

'Check them both out. See if they've got alibis or if there's any sign of radicalisation.'

'I think it's something more personal,' Harrison spoke now, and the room turned to look at him.

DCI Turner raised an eyebrow as if to question his interruption, and in a slightly mocking tone introduced him to the team. 'This is Harrison Lane, a profiler who has been sent from the National Crime Agency.'

Harrison didn't show a flicker of reaction on his face.

'I'm head of the Ritualistic Behavioural Crime Unit – I'm a psychologist and expert in religious and ritualistic crime. The manner of Reverend Soulsby's death suggests a far more personal motive. He has been flogged, which indicates that his murderer feels he needs to atone for a sin. There's evidence of razor blades in his mouth which to me suggests the killer thinks he was lying or saying things which have hurt others. Then there's the sheep. These are indicative of his congregation and the murderer's view that they followed him blindly like sheep. The killer took a great deal of care with all of this. There's something deep-rooted and personal behind it.'

'Surely the razors in the mouth and the sheep could be motivated by the murderer's anger at the church's attempt to encourage more people to join their congregation, and Reverend Soulsby could have just been collateral damage?' DCI Turner challenged. 'Whoever has done this is angry at the church, or else why burn down the buildings?'

'They're angry at the church as an institution. Possibly because it has given protection to Reverend Soulsby and whatever it is that they think he's done. They're burning its buildings to stop it from hiding others like him.'

'There have been no complaints made about Reverend Soulsby.' The DCI abruptly dismissed Harrison's suggestion. 'If he was having an affair or abusing anyone, then we will find out about it. We're doing all the background checks, Dr Lane. We know how to do our jobs.'

Harrison realised he'd get nowhere without further evidence. The detective chief inspector was becoming defensive and now was not the time to pick a public fight in their first briefing.

'What about how they got entry to the churches?' DS Howard spoke up, diffusing the tension. 'We know that Justin Black's keys were found in the main doors of All Saints – he had to unlock those doors. The side door was still locked when the fire brigade arrived. So how did they get access to set the fire? Doesn't this suggest that it could be an inside job?'

'Find out who has keys and who could get access to keys,'

the DCI replied. 'I want a list of potential suspects and motives on this board by tomorrow morning.'

Her eyes flicked to the back of the room as she said this, and her demeanour shifted – slightly. It was obvious that somebody she wanted to impress had entered the room.

'Sir,' she said, nodding at an older uniformed officer who stepped forward from the doorway.

'DCI Turner. Any progress?'

Harrison guessed this was Detective Superintendent Mark Ferry, who had requested the NCA's help.

'We have several lines of enquiry, sir,' she replied.

The DSU wouldn't need to read between the lines to know that meant they didn't yet have a clue.

'I want surveillance on all the remaining churches in our districts. We've got the budget go ahead. They've hit two heritage sites in two nights. I don't want to lose a third this evening.'

'Absolutely. I'll make the arrangements.'

Ferry's eyes did a quick scan of the room. 'Dr Lane?' he asked.

'Yes.' Harrison stood up and moved forward, his hand outstretched.

'Thank you for coming to assist. This is a dire situation we find ourselves in and any expert help is much appreciated.'

Harrison tipped his head in reply.

The DSU then said to the room, 'I want to thank you all for getting this enquiry going so quickly. I know it's been fast-moving and we have a lot of pressures, but I'm sure you will all do your utmost to stop this murder and destruction in our community. Thank you.' He had clearly gone to a different school of leadership to DCI Turner.

He looked back at DCI Turner and said, 'Call me day or night with updates or if you need any further resources,' before turning with one final nod and leaving the incident room.

'You heard the boss,' DCI Turner said. 'Let's get to work.'

She sat down and turned her attention to her computer screen. The room immediately erupted into activity and noise. DS Howard slipped into the chair next to Harrison.

'Going to be a long night,' he said, sighing.

'I'm going to head out to All Saints,' Harrison replied in response. He was still perplexed as to why that particular church had been burned down and yet nobody appeared to have been targeted. 'Who's the vicar of All Saints?' he asked the DS.

'They're waiting on a new one. Reverend Smith recently left to go on a mission to Africa. I believe that the other three vicars, Soulsby, Galloway, and Davenport, are all sharing the workload until a new one arrives.'

'So it's possible that the murderer went there thinking Martin Soulsby was going to be there too? Would there be a timetable for them?'

'Good point. I'll check it out.' DS Howard made a note on the pad next to him, adding it to a very long list, and then scrubbed at his face with his palms.

Harrison left him to it. It was going to be a very long night indeed.

12

DECEMBER 18TH

It was a fifteen-minute drive to All Saints from the incident room, which was long enough for Harrison to notice that the weather was starting to close in. The sky had turned to that dense dark gray colour which heralds snow clouds and there was scant evidence of wildlife. The birds and mammals were preparing to hunker down for the evening, finding somewhere to take shelter and keep warm. There'd be no lighting at the church, thanks to the fire, so he'd need to be quick if he was to take a look around before dusk fell.

The fire crews had finished up, their initial investigations complete, and a series of metal barriers had been erected around the walls of the burnt-out structure. The church stood on the outskirts of the village, stark and lonely against the fading light of the sky. Unlike St Luke's that morning, the crowd of onlookers had long gone. There was a small pile of flower bouquets and cards at the front porch. Tributes to Justin Black, the verger.

Harrison stopped for a moment to look at the cards.

Double-checking there weren't any that looked like they could be from the perpetrator. When he stood up again, he realised the place wasn't totally deserted. Just across the graveyard, a small man was working at clearing up some of the debris, one eye on Harrison.

The man wore a waterproof all-weather coat and a woollen hat, but no gloves. He was clearly used to being outdoors and wasn't as bothered about the cold as most people. He was also brushing and scraping at the debris between the gravestones and looked as though he had been doing it for a while. It would have helped keep him warm. Around him, the area was now cleared, a small refuge for the dead from the blackened detritus that smothered the entire site.

As Harrison approached him, the man looked down, trying to avoid eye contact.

'Hi,' Harrison said. 'I'm working with the police.' He took his ID card out to show the man. 'Dr Harrison Lane.'

'Doctor?' the man replied quietly and tipped his head up a couple of inches to look up at the big man in front of him.

Even with his face half hidden in his coat collar, it was clear why the man was shy. There were small lumps all over his face. Harrison wasn't a medical doctor, so he didn't know what had caused the lumps, but he could see more on the man's hands and guessed they were probably all over his body. They would inevitably have meant a lifetime of abuse and bullying.

It was difficult to tell the man's age – his hair was hidden under the black woollen beanie hat, but there was evidence of grey in the patchy stubble on his face. There were a couple of scars on one cheek, where it looked like some of the lumps may have been removed, and Harrison wondered if maybe he had an aversion to doctors. It would explain why he'd repeated Harrison's doctor title nervously.

Harrison tried to reassure him. 'I'm a doctor in psychology. Head of the Ritualistic Behavioural Crimes unit. I'm here to see if I can help with the attacks on the churches and murder of Reverend Soulsby.'

The man nodded. 'George,' he simply replied. 'The sexton. I already spoken to police. They got a statement. I told them I wasn't here when it happened.'

'I'd like to take a look around, if that's OK?' Harrison replied gently. The man was clearly used to being confronted. He was also clearly upset by the recent events. His tone was depressed. His shoulders slumped. And there was a sadness in his eyes that told of a job he loved, which was now in ruins.

'I can open it – we locked it up. Stop kids from getting in.'

'Was anything stolen, do you know?' Harrison asked, following George round to a large padlock on the fencing.

Experience had told him that he got far more out of talking to those who were close to something than reading a statement which had been coached by the officer taking it. Sometimes the official line of events took a set direction, and it was the little avenues off the main theories that gave you the gems you needed. If George worked at the church, he'd have seen and heard a lot of what had gone on before the fire, too.

'No. The cupboard with the valuables was still locked. The fire was in the vestry.'

'What about the graveyard? Were any graves disturbed or damaged?'

'No.'

George was a man with the same communication style as Harrison. He appreciated direct answers and knew that George would have checked every one of his tenants.

Inside the metal fencing, a perimeter of around three feet surrounded the whole building. It took in most of the path, which was still a quagmire of icy water, sandy gravel, and cinders. The main doors to the church were miraculously still standing, with no visible evidence of fire damage. If you kept your head at the right angle, and ignored your nose, then the doors and stone walls of the building could trick you into thinking that nothing had happened. It was only the ground and the roof which betrayed the truth. That and the pungent stench of burned wood.

George put his key in the lock to open up. As the door swung open, a disconcerting view met Harrison's eyes. Inside, the ceiling of the church was the sky, a void above their heads with nothing but the dark grey clouds giving a feeling of uneasy exposure. The building was a shell with only blackened ribs remaining to show where once a roof had been. The ground was a wet mush of charcoal and cindered wood. Here and there were markers left by Forensics, and it wasn't difficult to spot the area in which the unfortunate Justin Black had been found.

Harrison stood for a moment looking at the devastation. The only object still standing was a marble cross at the front of the church. Defiant but despairing. Black rivulets of water stained its white facade like devil's tears.

'You don't know anybody who would have wanted to do this?' Harrison asked George.

The sexton shook his head.

'And everywhere has been checked? There's nothing missing and nothing added?'

'No. The sacristy is through that door at the back. It was closed. The fire didn't get through.'

Harrison's eyes scanned the far end of the church, and the blackened door. It looked as though it had been minutes away from giving in to the flames. 'What about through there?' He nodded to George's right, where a smaller doorway was tucked away.

'That's the crypt.'

'But you checked?'

George shook his head. 'I think the fire crew went down.'

Harrison could tell by the hesitation in George's voice that the thought hadn't crossed his mind. He was probably in shock, faced with the devastation of the church. The fire investigation team would have sealed the site until they'd conducted their work. Their focus would have been on the valuables and paperwork in the back. After that, George would have quite reasonably assumed everywhere had been examined.

There might be nothing down in the crypt, but experience told Harrison that they needed to check every single possibility. Unless the person who set the fire did so just to watch a Christian church burn, there was no other motive apparent. Somehow Harrison couldn't marry that up to the well-planned and staged crime scene he'd seen that morning. There had to be an answer somewhere.

George rattled his keys, searching for the one that would open the crypt door. He pushed it into the lock and tried to turn the key.

'It's unlocked,' he said, frowning.

'Perhaps the fire crew left it unlocked?' Harrison offered.

The door didn't open easily, the hinges warped in the heat of the fire. Harrison stepped forward to help. He was concerned that the door might be too fragile and simply fall apart. The wood was blackened and there was no telling how deeply the flames had eaten into it. He gave it a wrench, enough to get it open an inch so that they could pull on the door itself and not the handle, which was only just hanging onto the wood. Finally, they dragged it open enough to allow them to enter.

George led the way down, using the small torch attached to his utility belt to light the steps. Harrison turned on his phone torch, and ducked to avoid the low stone lintel above it. The steps were also narrow, the whole structure definitely not designed for men of his height and bulk. It had a claustrophobic feel, heading underground in darkness, and Harrison had to push away a natural instinct of trepidation.

The stench of smoke had been trapped down here in the still air, and both men covered their nose and mouth as best as they could as they walked along a narrow tunnel with sealed burial chambers on either side, and then into a larger chamber at the end. Fire debris littered the floor from above. Around the chamber, stone shelves held wooden coffins which, amazingly, had not fallen victim to the flames.

George let out a gasp.

'The bishop!' he said and rushed forward towards an opened coffin.

Harrison followed in his wake.

'He's gone.' George spun round to Harrison, his eyes wide in shock. 'They've stolen his body.'

'Don't touch anything. We need to get Forensics down here,' Harrison warned him.

George scuttled backwards like a frightened pony.

'When was the last time you were down here?'

George's eyes searched around, looking for the answer in the gloom. 'A week ago. I come down regularly to check for vermin. It's dry and warm and in winter we get mice and rats setting up home down here.' His eyes fell on a mousetrap in the shadows of the far corner. It was unsprung.

'Would anyone else come down here?' Harrison questioned.

George shook his head and frowned. 'I don't think so.'

'Who was it that was in the coffin?'

'Bishop Peter Warriner. He was a vicar here for many years before eventually becoming bishop.'

'When did he die?'

'About two years ago.'

'And is it well known that he's here?'

'Oh yes. There was a big service.'

Harrison nodded thoughtfully and made a note of the bishop's name.

'Anything else missing?' he asked George.

'I don't think so. All the other coffins still look sealed.'

While George scanned the other inhabitants of the chamber, Harrison trained his phone torch on the ground and the area around the bishop's coffin. The floor was stone and so unlikely to offer up any footprints and besides, they'd have been covered by the film of soot which had settled everywhere. All he could see were George's and his own traces.

Carefully, he edged forward and peered inside the coffin. There was something still inside. He angled his phone to shine the light right into the interior and illuminated three finger bones. One still wearing a ring. The bones showed white at the ends where they were once attached to the rest of the hand. These hadn't fallen off accidentally, they'd been cut.

He'd found their arsonist's motive. The next question was how did Bishop Warriner connect to Reverend Soulsby and why steal his body?

13

DECEMBER 18TH

The smell of burning hypocrisy was still in their nostrils. It was a shame to see the firefighters looking so exhausted and disappointed that they couldn't do more. None of this was their fault. The media had predictably been buzzing around like flies on rotting meat, but that wasn't a bad thing. They spread the word. Documented the demise of these false evangelists. The reporters and their cameras would be there at the final reckoning, too. That was for sure.

There was at least some satisfaction that the news was now out about Bishop Warriner's missing corpse. With the death of Soulsby, would Reverend Davenport be putting two and two together now? If he had, what would he do? He couldn't go to the police. Perhaps he might arm himself. Take extra security precautions. It wouldn't matter. There would be no escape. Justice would be served.

St Mary's would be in flames and while the emergency services concentrated on putting out that fire, Reverend

Davenport would be having a little chat and sharing his final words.

14

———

DECEMBER 18TH

Harrison had called in the news about Bishop Warriner's corpse to DS Howard, who was quick to dispatch a forensic team to the scene. He waited for their arrival, keen to ensure that the coffin and fingers weren't touched. George and Harrison had retreated upstairs and back to the graveyard, away from the still air of the crypt. Keen to get some fresh oxygen in their lungs and not the acerbic stench of smoke.

George was upset at the latest development. While waiting for the team, Harrison took the opportunity to ask him some questions. Get a feel for who the targets of their perpetrator's wrath had been.

'The bishop was a good man. Even when he was made bishop, he never forgot us here. It's wrong that his body has been defiled.'

'Do you know of anyone who didn't like the bishop? Perhaps was vocal about him when he was alive?'

George vehemently shook his head. 'He was respected. Loved.'

Harrison tried a different tack. George's rose-tinted glasses were unlikely to see any faults or any reason for someone to not feel as he did.

'What connections are there between All Saints and St Luke's churches?'

George looked at him with some surprise, as though it were a silly question.

'Well, they're both in the same diocese. The bishop looked after all the churches in this area. He appointed Reverend Soulsby.'

'Do the churches share vicars?'

'No. We have strong congregations. Each church has its own vicar. I'm the only staff member who works at both.'

'So you tend to the graveyard and manage the building maintenance at both churches?'

George nodded sadly. 'The bishop appointed me. My job is my life. Been here over forty years. I hope—' He didn't finish. A tear formed in his left eye and he turned away from Harrison.

'Who else has keys to the buildings besides yourself and the vicars?'

'The vergers. There are two at each church.'

'Justin Black was verger here?'

George nodded sadly again.

'Has there been any trouble in any of the graveyards of late? Any graves defiled?'

'No.'

'Any graves receiving flowers out of the blue, when there haven't been any visitors for a long time?'

George thought hard, then shook his head. The man looked beaten down. Forty years of caring for two properties which were now blackened wrecks, and, of course, the death of Justin Black, Reverend Soulsby, and now the removal of

Bishop Warriner. It was no surprise he was struggling with it all. Harrison made a mental note to flag up that he might need some support. It was obvious that he was a bit of a loner and he might not even have any family.

They heard a van pull up and feet scrunch up the gravel. The forensics team had arrived.

After he'd briefed the team, he headed back to his car. Tiredness was beginning to overwhelm him. It had been a long day of concentration and the smell of the smoke didn't help. It seeped into every pore of his body and settled there, smothering his skin with a layer of very fine charcoal ash. The thought of his hotel room and a hot shower had formed in his head and pulled at him like a Greek siren call. He was about to leave when DS Howard pulled up.

DS Howard looked tired. His eyes were red-rimmed and there were creases on his face, which hadn't been there that morning. Amazingly, however, his clothes were still absolutely perfect. His suit could have just been put on fresh.

'Can't believe nobody spotted this before,' he said as he reached Harrison. 'We sure it was done prior to the fire?'

'I believe so. The soot from the fire has covered everything. If it was done after the fire, then that would have been disturbed. It wasn't. The fire crews would have checked for anyone trapped or any signs of the fire having spread. It was just coffins down there.'

'Bizarre. And you say they've taken the body but left some fingers? Cut off the fingers or just accidentally left them behind?'

'Cut off. You can see the fresh cut marks.'

'So what the hell do they want with his corpse and why leave some fingers behind? And what does the bishop have to do with Reverend Soulsby?'

Harrison didn't answer the questions hanging between them. He couldn't. Not yet.

'I'm going to check into my hotel, get some thinking time. You've got my number.' Harrison said. He felt a bit guilty because the DS still probably had a few hours ahead of him.

'Yeah. Cheers. I checked out the rota for the vicars, by the way, and Soulsby hadn't been due here until next week. But I guess that's not important anyway as you've found the motive now. See you in the morning, Dr Lane.'

Harrison got into his car and drove away, leaving DS Howard to get an initial update from the forensics team. Behind him, the banner on the railings advertising the Christmas service times flapped impotently in the breeze.

THE HOTEL WAS a fifteen-minute drive from the village. Despite the freezing cold temperatures outside, Harrison opened the car's front windows in an attempt to blow away the stench of burning from his nostrils and his clothes. He was looking forward to getting in the shower and washing his hair and skin.

The hotel car park was busy, and he had to find a space round the back in their overflow car park. Women in sparkly party dresses and men in shiny suits were standing outside in the cold, jigging up and down on the spot to keep warm while they smoked a cigarette, or took a drag from e-cigs. Their breath rose as plumes in the cold air while they giggled and chatted conspiratorially. Office Christmas party season was in full flow.

The lobby of the hotel was a smorgasbord of OTT festive gaudiness. The most bling baubles he'd ever seen smothered an imitation tree which was surrounded by what were undoubtedly fake gifts, wrapped in bright metallic paper. A tacky Father Christmas and his elves were dotted across the reception desk. It was the opposite of the solemn religious rituals of the Christian celebration, and Harrison was reminded how Christmas meant different things to different people.

For some, it wasn't a celebration at all. One of the receptionists wore a traditional Muslim hijab. The Muslim community not only didn't celebrate Jesus's birthday, but they also didn't believe Christmas Day to be the day he was actually born. Harrison wondered what she thought about having to work amidst the plethora of tacky festive decorations, or having to listen to the over-sentimental Christmas songs which were being played endlessly through the speakers. They weren't even the original artists.

Harrison could see a couple of people walking from the restaurant to the toilets who looked as though they'd had a bit too much festive cheer already. He made the immediate decision that dinner would be in his room.

It felt good to close the hotel room door and feel the silence settle around him. As usual, Harrison ignored the TV and instead went straight to the bathroom and a hot shower. He stood for longer than necessary, washing the smell of fire from himself and allowing the warm water to flow across his muscles, easing the tensions of the day.

Afterwards, he tried to close his eyes and meditate for a few minutes, but he found the image of Reverend Soulsby and the crows etched into the back of his eyelids.

Harrison's body and mind were tired, but they were also hungry, and so he'd ordered himself some dinner. Perhaps if he had a big meal to digest, his body might turn its attention to his stomach and the food – and allow him some sleep.

While he waited for his meal, he called Ryan to see if he had anything to report, and to update him.

'Boss.' The familiarity of his assistant's voice was welcome.

'We've had another development. A corpse was taken from the first fire at All Saints, Bishop Warriner, who used to be a vicar at the church and later went on to lead the diocese. The two men have to be connected to our pyromaniac somehow.'

'He's taken his corpse?'

'Yeah. I think he's planning a trial.'

'How the hell do you put a corpse on trial?'

Ryan could still be surprised by some of the unusual cases they worked on.

'Well, it's a bit of a one-way conversation...' Harrison replied.

'Didn't give Reverend Soulsby much of a trial, did he? I'd say there was a bit more punishment and sentencing involved there.'

Harrison couldn't disagree.

'I've not got much so far. Just a couple of local news reports that a new age community had complained about the church's attempts to brainwash children at the village school. All pretty tame. Reading between the lines, I think the journalist was beefing it up a bit.'

'Mmmh, that's been mentioned.'

'Other than that, no obvious scandals or accusations, at least none that were made public.'

'Well, we know the Church look after their own. There's been enough public inquiries to prove that. We're going to need to dig deep into this one and see if anything has been buried.'

'Of course, boss.'

At that moment, a sharp knock sounded on Harrison's

hotel room door followed by a voice calling out, 'Room service.'

'That your in-room masseuse?' Ryan laughed.

'No! It's my dinner. I'll speak tomorrow,' Harrison replied. 'Night, Ryan.'

'Night, boss.'

RYAN ENDED the phone call to Harrison with a big smile on his face. His boss's complete inability to know how to handle jokes always amused him.

He looked at the time. It was gone 7 p.m., and he still hadn't gone downstairs to pick up his post. Although it was just a two-flight trip down the stairwell, it was still a journey he didn't enjoy. He'd only moved in a couple of weeks ago and new surroundings were always a challenge.

He opened his flat door and listened. It was quiet. A good chance he wouldn't bump into anyone and have to strike up a conversation and stay out longer than he wanted. Slowly, Ryan edged down the stairs, concentrating on keeping his breathing steady and reminding himself that he was just a few feet away from his flat door.

At the bottom, he unlocked his mailbox and found a single, official-looking envelope. Probably one of the utility companies contacting him. Ryan turned to start making his way back to safety, and had just put his foot on the first step when one of the flat doors on the ground floor was flung open.

An Asian man walked out, looking at his phone. He was fit and toned, with an extended goatee beard and street clothes that looked casual, but Ryan could tell they would have cost more than a week's salary for most people.

Ryan's heart leaped, and his stomach flipped. He tried to

walk up the stairs quickly, turning his head away from the man, but it was too late.

'Chapman? Yo, Chapman! Where you been, bro?'

Ryan froze. Should he keep on going and pretend he hadn't heard him, or that he was mistaken? His feet kept on walking.

'Chapman.' The call came again, only this time it was closer. The man had started to come up the stairs after him. He felt his hand on his arm.

There was nothing for it but to brazen it out.

Ryan turned. 'Addie! Mate, didn't realise it was you.'

'Where's you been, bro? You took off when all the beef went down.'

'Yeah. Lying low.'

'This your ends now, man?'

'Err, no. Just visiting.'

'Why you got post?' Addie nodded at the letter in Ryan's increasingly sweaty hand.

He always had been a smart arse.

'Yeah, I mean, I'm just staying here a short while, you know.'

'Cool. Me woman lives there.' Addie nodded to the door he'd just exited. 'Gotta shift. Got a meetin' with a face. I'll see ya around, yeah.'

With that, Addie turned and headed out the front door, leaving Ryan frozen in fear on the stairs.

They'd found him again. There was no chance Addie was going to leave it there. He'd immediately be on the phone to tell them their tech guru was back. He'd never be able to escape the gang a second time. This time, they'd make sure they didn't lose him.

15

DECEMBER 18TH

There were a lot of advantages to having insider knowledge, and one of them was knowing the remaining churches in the area were being watched. It would make things a bit trickier, but it wasn't an insurmountable issue. Some of the oldest tricks in the book were the best. The Greeks had it sussed centuries ago. The Trojan Horse worked then and it would work tonight.

St Mary's was a hive of activity. There had been a lot of coming and going throughout the day as valuable documents and silverware from both All Saints and St Luke's were brought over to be stored here and at St Peter's. The community had pulled together and unwittingly provided the perfect cover for the next stage of the plan.

Reverend Edward Davenport seemed to be enjoying the increased bustle at his church, possibly in part because he felt safer in a crowd. It wouldn't have escaped his notice that there was a possibility he might be next, but then maybe he was arrogant enough to think he hadn't done anything wrong. That would be his downfall.

One of the local schools was holding their end of term carol service in the early evening, and it posed the perfect opportunity for a little distraction. Over a hundred parents, young children, and local dignitaries could be a very effective cover.

They were about halfway through the service when the small explosion happened. It was at the perfect moment, during a period of quiet prayer, when the congregation was mostly silent. Within seconds, they had erupted.

Reverend Davenport, the vergers, several members of the congregation, and a police officer who'd been stationed inside all instantly jumped into action. Before the panic could cause a stampede, they had the church doors open at the back and were asking everyone to evacuate calmly. They helped mothers with small children, grandparents with mobility issues, and within just a few minutes, everyone was out. It was an impressive operation, backed up by several squad cars of police who had descended on the church to find out what had caused the explosion. Purple smoke could be seen coming from the sacristy, and the fire engines were en route.

Outside, many of the families disappeared quickly, keen to get their children to safety. But as is typical of human nature, many more stayed to watch. Locals from the village who came rushing to see the commotion joined them. A crowd of around fifty quickly swelled to well over a hundred and the police officers battled to push them away from the crime scene in order to allow the fire crews access.

In the dark, frightened faces looked on as flames started to appear from the side of the church. Who needed to be at home watching TV when they had the real thing? While all eyes were focused on St Mary's, luring Reverend Davenport away unseen had been easy. The fool came willingly. A lamb to the slaughter. He was actually quite scared. Aware that he might be the next target, he'd trusted his companion to get him to safety.

The minute they were alone, it had been even easier to trick him into handing over his mobile phone. The second that the investigation team realised the vicar was missing, they'd try to trace him with his phone signal. As it went out the window of the car into a roadside ditch, the realisation that he was in danger set in.

'What are you doing? Where are you taking me?'

'Just for a little drive and a chat. There's nothing to worry about.'

Reverend Davenport's face and the whites of his eyes showed that he didn't believe the lie. So, he did what he always did: tried to talk his way out of it. Tried to lie too.

'I'm not sure what you are doing and why, but we can sort this out between us if you just stop the car and allow me to answer whatever misunderstanding has happened. Our Lord teaches forgiveness. Whatever you have done, we can work through it together. I will help you.'

The snigger that met his plaintive whining was not what the vicar hoped for.

'I don't forgive, though, Reverend Davenport – and I stopped listening to your Lord a long time ago. If you're honest, so did you. It's time that you paid for the sin you committed. We will indeed work together to help you do just that.'

'I don't know what you're talking about. I've done nothing. I have served my church and my community all of my life.'

'Don't worry, I have an idea for a little game that will help jog your memory. It will also help bring you closer to your Lord Jesus. He suffered for you by being nailed to the cross.

I've got a slight twist to that story for you. You'll have the chance to tell me the truth, but I don't want to be too long with this. I need to get back before I'm missed, so the quicker we can get to the answer, the better.'

EYES WIDE, Reverend Edward Davenport looked at the interior of the car they were in. He'd not seen the car before; an old Ford. Not their usual vehicle. Why hadn't he noticed that before he got in? He'd been so shocked by the night's events that all his common sense had gone out the window. He stared silently ahead into the darkness, knowing the answer that was being sought and trying to work out if it could save him.

They'd not driven far from the village before they turned off the road. It wasn't somewhere that Reverend Davenport had visited, but he knew there was just one business at the end of this track: a scrapyard. What were they going down here for? Were they going to change cars and drive on?

Discreetly he looked around the car, searching for anything he could use as a weapon to defend himself, but there was nothing. He was alone and unarmed. Panic rose in his throat, creating a tight knot of sickness.

As they pulled into the scrapyard, the only light was the car headlights and a Father Christmas smothered in multi-coloured fairy lights that seemed to be hanging mid-air, high above them with a sign that flashed Merry Christmas. Just across the row of trees which ran down the side of the yard was the main A143 road. If he could just get away, then he might be able to get help. There were always cars passing along the road at regular intervals.

'I want you to put your hands behind your back,' his

captor said, producing a plastic bag with pull ties. 'Come on now, we need to get a move on. Remember?'

It was a strange thing, but, when faced with no options, you tended to do as you were told in the hope it might stop something even worse happening. Reverend Davenport undid his safety belt and twisted in his seat. He was about to put both hands behind his back when he came to his senses and lurched at the car door release. It was locked.

'I don't think so, Reverend.'

He felt a hand hit the back of his head and slam his forehead into the side window.

'I fixed the door to ensure it had a child lock. Only way you're getting out is if I let you. Now, hands behind your back.'

The impact with the window had stunned him, but more frightening was the change in tone of his companion. There was no longer any pretence at friendship. He did as he was told this time, putting his hands behind his back and feeling the plastic ties tighten around his wrists. His heart was already beating so hard he thought it might burst out of his chest, but the touch of the latex gloves on his skin sent it roaring even faster. He knew what they meant. They had no intention of letting him leave alive.

'You have to at least give me a chance to defend myself. To answer whatever it is you think that I've done. I've got a wife and children,' he said, a little fight returning to him. He turned and looked into eyes of cold steel.

'Do you remember what Bishop Warriner asked you to do forty years ago? You hid a crime and didn't help a vulnerable young woman who was the victim. Instead, you tried to cover it up. Remember that?'

He shook his head, but his stomach betrayed him first and he nearly vomited all over the car.

'I want to know the name of the perpetrator. But first you've got some hard truths to swallow.'

Reverend Davenport watched as a bag of nails was produced. His skin shivered at the possibility that these were about to be hammered into his flesh.

'As I said, we're going to have a slight twist on the crucifixion. You took her to have her insides butchered. I'm going to repay the favour. You're going to swallow these. Then we will see whether your memory can be jogged.'

16

DECEMBER 18TH

Harrison had lain down on the bed after his room service dinner and begun to process through all the evidence he'd seen that day. Some elements were clear to him. He was convinced that the motivation came from a deep-seated personal need for revenge. There was too much time and detail put into the murder for it to be a random act or one that was purely an institutional-based target.

The use of the clay dolls and fire also suggested clues as to how the killer viewed themselves and the world. It was quite possible that the thirst for revenge had now been sated with the murder of Reverend Soulsby. But the taking of Bishop Warriner's body indicated otherwise. If it was just to satisfy a personal score against the two men, then why not defile the bishop's body there and then? Why take it away? Harrison feared there was more to come.

His mobile phone woke him. He was still lying on top of the bed, wrapped in a towel, and must have slipped asleep through sheer exhaustion. When he saw DS Howard's name appear on the phone screen, he knew his fears were about to be realised.

'Dr Lane. They've struck again. There was a fire at St Mary's. We've managed to get it under control quite quickly, but Reverend Edward Davenport is missing. We're searching for him now.' Both fear and weariness were evident in the DS's voice.

'I'll be there right away,' Harrison said, springing from the bed. Thinking about the likelihood of further smoke, he threw the day's charcoal-scented clothes back on. No point in ruining a fresh set of clothing.

IT HAD GONE 7 pm when he arrived at St Mary's and the crowds had thinned; the media were packing up their cameras, and the fire brigade were starting to put away their hoses. A few portable generators were being used to light the scene for Forensics and the police investigation. Total disaster for the church had been avoided, but the concern was more for the vicar than the building. That last fact hadn't been communicated to the media – yet.

DCI Turner was standing shaking her head, talking to two men who Harrison vaguely recognised as having been at the St Luke's fire. One was a vicar and the other a smartly dressed middle-aged man. The DCI didn't see him and he wasn't about to draw attention to himself.

Harrison spotted DS Patrick Howard pacing up and down on his phone a few yards away, so he walked over and waited for him to finish.

'This is one hell of a crap storm!' DS Howard said to him the second he'd ended his call. His face showed the strain they were all under. 'We had officers watching the church. We even had one stationed inside. Seems there was a small explosion during a school carol concert, and then a fire in the side room. Everyone got out safely and they managed to bring the fire under control, but during the mayhem Reverend Davenport disappeared. Nobody remembers seeing him after the church was evacuated. He just disappeared.'

Harrison looked towards the church and saw the fire chief heading their way.

'DS Howard,' the fire chief tipped his head at the DS. 'Initial thoughts, and only initial obviously because we need to run tests: it looks like a device had been rigged in a box. From the reports of purple smoke, we're thinking possibly potassium chlorate. It's a common-enough experiment that science teachers do to impress the kids. Looks like it was in one of the boxes brought over this afternoon from the other churches.'

'So, different from the other two blazes?'

'Yes, but perhaps they knew that the churches were being watched and had to come up with a workaround,' Harrison offered.

'You could well be right,' the fire chief agreed. 'And if I'm right about the chemicals used, they're not hard to come by. We aren't talking some sophisticated incendiary device or the hallmark of a terrorist attack. It was never going to do as much damage as pouring diesel over everything.'

'OK, thank you,' DS Howard replied, just as his phone began to ring. He picked up and listened.

'We've got a location on Reverend Davenport's phone. A team's out searching for it now,' he said to Harrison when he finished the call.

'So the primary aim was to get to the vicar, not burn down the church,' Harrison suggested.

DS Howard thought for a moment. 'It would look that

way, wouldn't it? But we can't be sure. Not until the fire investigation team has finished. Maybe the device didn't go off as planned. We've not found a clay doll yet either. We could be panicking over nothing. Maybe the vicar's gone to ground somewhere, terrified that he was going to be the next victim.' But Harrison could tell from Patrick's face that he didn't believe that and it was wishful thinking.

His phone rang again. 'OK. Yeah,' he spoke into it.

It was obvious it wasn't good news.

'Reverend Davenport's phone's been found in a ditch on the way out of the village. We've got no way of tracing him. If he was taken away in a car, he could be anywhere by now.' Patrick kicked at the ground with his polished black leather shoes and swore.

'Do you know who that is talking to the DCI?' Harrison asked him.

The pair of them looked over to where the DCI was now chatting to just one of the men Harrison had seen earlier.

'Yes, that's Reverend Galloway.'

'He was at the St Luke's fire,' Harrison noted, keen to see the DS's reaction.

'They were all his colleagues. If we don't find Reverend Davenport, then he's the only one left. If I were him, I'd be hanging around wherever the police are, too.'

Harrison looked around the area, keen to see if he could spot signs of how Edward Davenport had left the church. He found nothing.

The church was sat in the middle of the village. It was surrounded by houses and with the congregation all evacuated and emergency service personnel swarming over the area, there should have been plenty of witnesses if he'd been dragged away under duress. As with Reverend Soulsby, there'd been no signs of a struggle. Harrison was convinced the men knew their killer.

A shadow creeping through the graveyard caught Harrison's eye. It was George, the sexton. He intercepted him.

'George,' Harrison greeted him. 'Do you work at this church, too?'

George looked startled and decidedly uncomfortable at the question. He nodded while staring at the ground and clutching at the toolbox he had in his hands.

'Anything you've noticed that's different apart from the fire?'

George shook his head. 'It's not as bad as St Luke's and All Saints. We'll be able to repair it.'

Harrison suspected that he hadn't been told about the missing vicar.

'Were you at the carol service?'

George shook his head again.

'The verger rang me. Said they might need to secure the church overnight. I brought my tools.' George lifted up his toolbox as if Harrison hadn't already noticed it.

'OK, I won't hold you up, but if you notice anything different, let me know.'

George nodded his head, eager to get away, and quickly shuffled off.

With nothing more that he could do, Harrison eventually returned to his hotel room. Patrick and his team would no doubt be up at least half the night trying to find the missing vicar. He hoped that it would turn out that the man had just panicked and hidden, but the last two days told him that this was unlikely.

Harrison was exhausted, but sleep was harder to come his way than earlier. He eventually drifted off around 1:30 a.m.

Thoughts whirled around his mind and a knot in his gut told him that tomorrow he'd be viewing another corpse.

17

DECEMBER 19TH

Charlie Cooper arrived at his salvage yard at about the same time as the first phone calls were being received by the local police. Later, he found out that most were people complaining about his festive display, totally unaware of what they were looking at.

'It's more like something from Halloween than Christmas,' the first female caller had said. 'My kids were upset.' A couple of others who had never been Charlie's biggest fans were less polite with their comments. The police said they'd look into it, but a festive decoration was hardly high on their priority list. Not with a church burning murderer on the loose.

It was true: Charlie Cooper hadn't always lived his life on the right side of the law, but he'd mellowed with old age. All he'd been trying to do was spread a bit of Christmas cheer. The sight which met his eyes when he arrived at his yard was anything but cheerful. It was also something he would never forget.

The first thing he'd noticed was that the blow-up Father

Christmas, which had been attached to the crane, was sitting in the middle of the yard. Next to it was a smaller object, which looked like some kind of pottery garden ornament. From his truck, he couldn't see the top of the crane and so he'd had to get out of his cab to be able to look up and work out what had gone wrong. At this point, he was oblivious to the phone calls to the police, and so he assumed it had somehow broken free of its mooring and fallen down. He was about to walk over and pick it up when a droplet splashing onto the plastic Father Christmas caught his eye. Instantly he noticed there were dark puddles around it and the white face was streaked with crimson. He instinctively looked up. Afraid.

Suspended on the large magnet, which was used to pick up the cars, was a terrible sight. He'd no idea who it was, but he knew it was the body of a human being wearing a Christmas hat, and blood was dripping from it.

Charlie Cooper staggered back to lean against the bonnet of his truck. He felt a pain in his chest as he fumbled for his mobile phone. The pain was sharper than he'd had before and he felt it travel down into his arm and up into his jaw. He dialled 999 and breathlessly called for the police and an ambulance. Then Charlie Cooper slid down the bonnet and onto the ground, clutching his chest and staring at the horrific spectacle in front of him.

By the time Harrison arrived, the yard was jam-packed with emergency service personnel, and the forensics team was just unpacking their van. He got out of his car and stopped a moment to look at the environment. They were in a large, wire fence-enclosed scrapyard. All down the left side were cars in various states of disrepair. Some had clearly been in accidents, their lids cut off by the fire crews trying to rescue the occupants. A pickup truck was parked under a carport-style structure. No doubt called out regularly to collect those vehicles destined for the crushing machine.

The only other building on the site was a scruffy-looking Portakabin with the sign: Office. Along the right-hand side were a few more cars, but also a great deal of other human detritus. Scrap fridges, washing machines, oil drums, and all manner of twisted bits of metal. At the back was the crusher. A big yellow metal box which would take a car and turn it into a handy cube size. There were examples of its produce lying on the ground near to it. The scrap yard was small scale compared to some of the big municipal ones, but no doubt still provided a good income for its owner.

Charlie was, however, going to have to take some time off from running the business. He was in an ambulance being treated for a minor heart attack. While the Reverend Davenport's demise had been incredibly unfortunate, Mr Cooper had been lucky. The medics told Harrison that Charlie's heart was in such bad shape that had he carried on for a few more weeks, he might not have recovered from a heart attack. Charlie Cooper was about to be taken off for emergency bypass surgery which meant he would get to live to see his grandson born.

As for Reverend Davenport, he was well and truly dead long before the morning light had risen. Once the paramedics and police had worked out how to bring him down from the top of the crane without just turning off the magnet and letting him drop, they quickly discovered there was nothing they could do to help him. The pathologist was just finishing up his initial inspection as Harrison approached.

'How the hell was he suspended up there?' DS Howard was asking the pathologist.

The pathologist was a very tall, lean man who would not do well to live in an old cottage with oak beams and low ceilings. He also no doubt struggled to fold himself into cinema and theatre seats, and would definitely need the extra leg room on an airplane. He had the pale, almost sallow skin of someone who spent most of their time inside and away from natural light. The periorbital edema, or puffy eyes to the non-medics, that Harrison noted he suffered with, also didn't help: the bags under his eyes made him look as though he was permanently tired.

'Unbelievably, I think it's nails.'

'Nails?'

'Yes, look. There's evidence of his skin being pierced by nails, but not from the outside. These are nails on the inside being forced outwards by the draw of the magnet.'

'An inside-out crucifixion,' Harrison said aloud.

The two men turned to look at him.

'Yes. So it appears,' the pathologist replied, raising his eyebrows and pressing his lips together in thought. 'It would have been an incredibly painful death unless he'd been lucky that one pierced his heart or a vital organ early on. There's evidence on both sides of his body. Whoever did this must have picked him up by his front initially. Then, once the nails had been drawn that way, they turned him over and picked him up by his back so they travelled back through the tissue again.'

'Christ,' DS Howard exclaimed.

'Exactly,' the pathologist remarked. 'I'm almost done with Reverend Soulsby. I'll get onto Reverend Davenport straight away and have more for you this afternoon. You'll be running out of vicars soon if they keep on turning up on my examination table.'

DS Howard sighed. 'Thanks, doc.' He then turned to Harrison. 'What sick animal does this to somebody?'

The two men watched as a forensics officer covered the former vicar's hands with plastic bags to preserve evidence. There was always the hope that he'd somehow got some of his killer's DNA under his fingernails.

'Someone very driven by a personal vendetta. How did they get him here?'

'We think we've got tyre prints over there, and we're checking if there's any CCTV between here and the village, but we've not found any so far. It's mostly country roads and woodland. We did get a report of a car found burnt out in the woods in between here and St Mary's. We need to see if that's related, but as you know, it won't be easy. Any forensic evidence is likely to be destroyed.'

'So the killer could have gone back into the village afterwards,' Harrison said.

'Yeah. If it's the vehicle they used, they could have.'

'And the yard doesn't have any security?'

'Just a padlock and that had been cut off. No CCTV. Difficult to find anything of value to nick from here.'

The sound of a car roaring into the yard made them turn their heads to a thunder-faced DCI Turner scowling through the windscreen.

'Great. Now she's going to be on our backs,' Patrick whispered to Harrison as she stomped towards them.

'Ma'am,' he said aloud and forced a smile.

'How the hell did they manage to kidnap and murder Reverend Davenport? Where was the surveillance team?'

'As you know, ma'am, there was a small explosion and fire in the church, and over a hundred young children and their families inside. The priority was getting everyone out safely and it appears that somewhere in that evacuation operation, the vicar went missing.'

'It might indicate that he knew his kidnapper,' Harrison added. 'There were too many people there – if Reverend Davenport had been forcibly taken, surely he'd have put up a fight bearing in mind recent events?'

'Thank you, Dr Lane. We are quite capable of drawing investigative conclusions without your input – even if we seem unable to protect a valuable member of our community.' She shot a venomous look at DS Howard. 'What a bloody mess. I'm going to get it in the neck. Did you know there are photos of him hanging up there on Twitter and TikTok? I hope somebody has informed his family?'

'Yes, ma'am, we have a Family Liaison with them now.'

'Get those photos taken down. And I want a full briefing in one hour. This has got to end.'

The DCI turned to leave just as a forensics officer approached her.

'Ma'am, I've just found this. It's a ticket with a seat number on it, so you might be able to trace who bought it.'

The DCI snatched the evidence bag from the forensics officer and peered at its contents.

Harrison could see it was a classical music concert ticket for seat six. It was subtle, but he saw a change in her face. Then she switched on her charm offensive.

'I'm so sorry to waste your time. It's mine. A lovely concert at the town hall. Must have blown out of my car as I got out. Apologies.' She smiled.

Harrison was reminded of a cartoon he'd watched once when he was a kid. A horrible woman wearing a big fur coat who was trying to deceive a nice woman because she wanted to steal her Dalmatian puppies to turn them into another coat. He seemed to remember her name was Cruella. It fitted the DCI perfectly.

Before the forensics officer could respond, DCI Turner had shoved the bag and ticket into her pocket and then returned her attention to DS Howard.

'Remember, one hour.'

With that, she was gone, leaving the three of them in her wake.

The forensics officer was clearly nonplussed, but went back to work. Heavily out-ranked.

Harrison said nothing, but he could see the DS was also surprised by the DCI's behaviour.

Harrison took out his phone and made a note of the concert name and the seat number. Something told him this might be useful.

THE INCIDENT ROOM resembled a frenetic ant colony under attack. There were phones ringing, people shouting instructions and information across the room to each other, and fingers tapping on keyboards. Harrison found the desk he had been sitting at occupied by a young woman who was clearly immersed in whatever work she was doing. He chose instead to stand at the back and wait for the briefing to begin.

The DCI was late and the scowl on her face seemed to have somehow embedded deep into the foundations of her features. She positively stomped into the room and officers moved away from her as though she was a repelling magnet.

'Briefing. Now!' she shouted, and the room fell silent as people returned to desks or took up a suitable position to watch.

'How did Reverend Davenport get kidnapped under our

noses? Who is going to be first with that one?' She scanned the room, eyes blazing. 'The detective superintendent had asked us to keep a watch on the churches and the ministers, and we failed on both counts. There will be some kind of inquiry. Heads will roll. But for now, I want to know what the hell happened.'

A uniformed officer was brave enough to speak up. 'Ma'am, Reverend Davenport was at the school carol service last night, along with around one hundred and twenty young children and community officials in the audience. It was around halfway through the service that a small explosion happened in a side room and a successful and orderly evacuation of the building was undertaken. Fire crews were promptly on the scene and the fire was brought under control quickly. Nobody received any injuries.'

'That wasn't what I asked,' the DCI bellowed.

'No, ma'am. I was explaining the situation,' he replied incredibly patiently.

Harrison could just see the officer's jawline tightening as he clenched his teeth to keep calm.

'The police personnel at the scene were prioritising public safety. Around half of the occupants of the carol service stayed to watch, and they were joined by a considerable number of villagers who were alerted to the emergency. We believe it was at some point during the attempt to push the public back to safety and allow the fire crews through that the vicar went missing. Eyewitnesses report seeing him up to this time. We do have some reported sightings later on, but we don't think these are Reverend Davenport. All officers have been through their bodycam footage, and we are continuing to make inquiries with the public in case anybody saw anything.'

'Where are we on suspects?' The DCI turned round to the board. 'What about the druid group in the forest?'

'I'm going to speak to them today, ma'am,' DS Howard spoke up.

'We're cross-referencing all those who had involvement with all three churches to see if there are any connections,' another officer added.

'Forensics?' the DCI barked back.

A middle-aged woman in a fuchsia-pink jumper raised her arm. 'Highlights of our report so far: there were no finger-prints found on any surfaces at the first two churches, including the coffin of the late bishop, so we can safely say the perpetrator was wearing gloves. We also can't find any DNA evidence on the clay figures they left behind. I'd say whoever is doing this is forensically aware. There is a clue in the fire accelerant they used. It was red diesel, which is only used around here by farmers.'

'Or municipal vehicles,' someone interjected. 'Gritters, snow ploughs, ride-on mowers and the like can use red diesel.'

'Check to see if any has been stolen and cross reference anyone who was at yesterday's carol service who might have access to any. And anyone with connections to all three churches,' DCI Turner ordered the officer, who nodded in reply. 'We don't believe the church doors were forced at All Saints, so it could be an insider job.'

'Reverend Soulsby's clothing indicates that he'd been made to carry the wooden sheep across the field,' the foren-sics officer continued.

'Like Jesus was forced to carry the cross to his crucifixion,' the DCI added. 'Anything else?'

'They're smart and don't leave much behind.'

'Great, so we're looking for a smart individual who knows how to evade a bunch of witless police officers. That should reduce the potential suspect list.'

The bitter sarcasm made the forensics officer sigh and sit down.

'Do we have a pathology report yet?' the DCI continued, oblivious.

'Dr Charles is in with Reverend Davenport, but has sent through some initial findings with regard to Reverend Soulsby,' DS Howard said. 'He died from a combination of shock, hypothermia, and blood loss. There were razors in his mouth which had cut his tongue and throat and some sort of whip with razors attached had been used across his back. No defensive wounds. The ties around his wrists were clean apart from his own DNA.'

'What time did he die?'

'He estimates some time around midnight.'

'So he would have seen his church on fire. We were just a few hundred yards away from him.'

The DS nodded.

'Dr Charles also said that Bishop Warriner's three fingers were cut with some kind of metal implement: heavy-duty wire-cutters, he's thinking.'

'So why cut off just those three fingers?' the DCI asked the room.

'The Cadaver Synod of 897,' Harrison spoke up, causing a room full of heads to swivel to the back.

'What?' the DCI asked incredulously.

'In 897, Pope Formosus was put on trial after his death. His cadaver was exhumed, tried and found guilty. The three fingers of its right hand were cut off because those were the fingers he'd used for blessings. It was his accuser's way of invalidating all his living acts and ordinations.'

'You're telling me that some ancient, dead Pope is being used as a template by our killer?'

'In this case, I'd say yes. As I said yesterday, I believe this to be a deeply personal and well-planned attempt to get justice for something the killer believes has been sinned against him or her, or someone close to them. Reverend Soulsby was forced to do penance before his death with flogging. Reverend Davenport, crucified inside out. There is something that all these three men were involved in and which relates to the perpetrator.'

'You're not falling back on the easiest to pick motive, are you, Dr Lane? Child abuse within the church. Is that what you're suggesting?'

'I'm not suggesting that, although it should be considered. I'm saying that whoever is doing this believes that the Church, through the men who served in it, has wronged them. Not only that, but the clay dolls, the act of setting fire to the churches, these are all indications of the ancient pagan winter solstice customs and Roman Saturnalia celebration. Our modern Christian Christmas festival replaced these. Even the Bible doesn't have Jesus's birth as the twenty-fifth of December, and indeed there is much evidence to indicate that couldn't have been the date. The killer seems to be pointing out that the Church took over and subsumed the original festivities, perhaps making a point about the falsehood of it all. It's about lies and coverups.'

'Well, that's a very dramatic theory, Dr Lane,' the DCI scoffed.

'It's not just a theory. It's there in the evidence. The methods of murder and what they leave behind.'

'Or it could just be a church-hating killer who is using religious metaphors for their crimes.'

Harrison shook his head. 'I believe that we haven't heard

the last from the killer. It's the nineteenth of December today. Tomorrow night is the eve of winter solstice and I think that could be their grand finale.'

'You *think*.' The DCI folded her arms across her chest.

'And how did our killer get into the sacristy to set off the explosion? If the church was being watched inside and out?'

'Initial indications are that it was a rudimentary device using potassium chlorate and some sulphuric acid that burned through and caused the explosion,' DS Howard said. 'It was in one of the boxes brought over during the afternoon from the other two churches, which had been burnt.'

'So you're saying it could have gone off at any time?'

'No. It was devised to go off at some point that evening, although it wouldn't have been an exact time.'

'So somebody who was helping with the boxes could have planted it?'

'That's the theory we're working on, ma'am.' DS Howard nodded.

'How many people are we talking about who would have had access?'

'Around a dozen.'

'A dozen. That could have given someone an opportunity to slip in during the removals.'

'Possibly.'

'This is not good enough. I have to give a press conference in a few hours and I want to report progress. Instead, I'm going to have to explain how my officers let a killer slip through their fingers right in front of their eyes. We could have had young children injured or killed. And all you're giving me is possibilities and maybes, or dramatised historical stories that may or may not be motives. And in the meantime, we have more clergy being murdered and churches being damaged. We need some firm progress. Do you all hear?'

The room murmured, 'Yes, ma'am.'

'Well, what are you waiting for? If you've got a list of a dozen people, go through every single one of them and make sure you've turned their lives upside down.'

18

DECEMBER 19TH

Harrison wasn't going to rise to the DCI's put down of him, or to her bullying behaviour. While she might be the lead investigating officer, she wasn't his boss. He felt positively sorry for Patrick and his colleagues, who weren't quite so lucky.

DS Howard walked across the room to Harrison once the briefing was over. 'Sorry about that,' he said to him.

'You don't need to keep apologising for her,' Harrison replied. 'Are you heading out to speak to the druid group now?'

The DS nodded.

'I'll tag along.'

'I was hoping you were going to say that. We need to be quick because it's started snowing and I don't fancy being stuck down the end of a dirt track with a bunch of pagans. Don't want to end up being burned like some wicker man for a druid solstice celebration,' DS Howard replied.

Harrison looked at him and was relieved to see he was joking.

'Can you tell me some more about your theory on the way?' the detective asked, smiling.

Harrison was amazed that the man could still be so cheerful working for a boss like Turner.

As THEY LEFT the station and got into DS Howard's car, the flurries of snowflakes were beginning to turn into a steady stream.

'This is all we need, the weather closing in on us now,' Patrick muttered. 'So explain to me this solstice theory.'

'The winter solstice was celebrated for centuries,' Harrison said, settling in for a long explanation. 'It goes back to early farming communities worshiping the sun and moon. At the winter solstice, the days are at their shortest and the nights their longest. It was the astronomical first day of winter and celebrations involved fire and light to celebrate the death and rebirth of the sun, as after the solstice the daylight hours get longer again. There's also one to mark the start of summer.

'It goes back to when humans totally relied on nature to be kind to their crops. It wasn't just our culture; the Romans had a god called Saturnalia who brought agriculture and civilisation when he arrived in Italy and again they celebrated him with a festival of light and lots of feasting. Then along came the Christians.

'If you look in the Bible, there's no mention of a date for when Jesus was born. In fact they talk of lambs in the fields and shepherds sleeping outside, and the eating of fresh dates. These events couldn't have taken place on the twenty-fifth of December. But about three centuries after his death, the Church declared it as his birthday. The Christian church took many of the original non-Christian holidays as their own.

Halloween is another one – that was a Celtic and Gaelic pagan harvest festival originally to celebrate that year's crops and mark the start of the darker part of the year.'

'But you said tomorrow night is the eve of the solstice?'

'Yes it is – now. Originally, the Romans celebrated it on the twenty-fifth. Over time, calendars have shifted.'

'OK, but what does that have to do with what's going on here?'

'I think our killer believes they've been wronged by members of the clergy. They're setting fire to the churches as a way to start again and cleanse – a kind of rebirth if you like, just like the original fire festivals. The clay dolls are sigillaria, which were the gifts given at the Saturnalia festival. They're highlighting how Christianity has usurped other original festivals, covering up their original meaning. As I said, it's all about lies and untruths.

'I think the red diesel and connection to these festivals indicate our perpetrator has links to farming; it's all tied to the land. They're smart, forensically aware, and obviously with local knowledge. From the footprints and gait in the field at All Saints, I'd say they're a little over six feet in height. Difficult to tell the build because the vicar was carrying the wooden sheep, so I can't directly compare the depth of the prints. All I'd say is they're not heavily overweight and they're not stick thin. Average build is my estimation.'

'And we're definitely talking a lone killer in your view? I mean, the evidence seems to point to that.'

'From what I've seen, yes. That doesn't mean they're not being helped away from the crime scenes, but, on the face of it, they're alone.'

'I think you were right about them knowing the killer, too. There are no struggles, the two vicars met willingly with the perpetrator, who, as you say, must have excellent local knowledge, or even possibly be an insider in the church. We need to look more closely at the vergers.'

'I think that this has roots that go back a long way, so you're going to need to look at that list of a dozen suspects and check their entire life histories.'

'Well, I think we're wasting our time with this lot here – the Light Grove Druids have been living in these woods for about ten years now. They bought a few acres and set up temporary structures. To be honest, I don't see they've done any harm at all. The complaints that others mentioned in the briefing were just a few druid parents who had complained that their kids were being indoctrinated into Christianity at school. I don't think that's motive enough for what's been going on, but we have to check everything out. One of them might have turned their back on mainstream society because of a childhood trauma linked to the church.'

'Indeed. Everything needs to be considered,' Harrison replied, pleased that the DS wasn't someone who instantly laid blame on those who lived on the edges of society. He'd seen enough of that in his childhood.

THE SNOW WAS HITTING the windscreen steadily as they drove, meaning DS Howard had to strain to see past the constant barrage of white flakes that slid down the glass before being whisked away by the wipers.

'It's somewhere along here,' DS Howard said to Harrison, slowing down. 'Here we go, it's just a dirt track. Nothing else along here but their settlement.' He pulled off the tarmac country road and started on a bumpy trail that led straight into the trees.

The forest was an old one. Deciduous mixed in with only a few evergreens; not one of the new commercial timber plantations that had sprung up all over the country. Ancient English oaks, beech, hazel and birch which had once been found across the country, supporting wildlife and humans alike.

The journey was slow because the DS didn't want to wreck his car suspension in the potholes, but eventually some coloured tents, old camper vans and temporary wooden structures came into view. There was nobody to be seen at first, until the flap on the largest tent flicked open and a man with long hair and a beard peered out at the newcomers.

He exited and closed the flap shut, no doubt keeping the cold out, and strode across to the car.

He was dressed in brightly coloured woollen trousers and a patchwork shirt, with beads around his neck and plaited into his beard, that was tinged with grey at its edge, almost as though it had always been like that.

Patrick got out of the car. 'Detective Sergeant Patrick Howard, we wondered if we could just have a chat.' He held his ID out to the man.

The man's face turned from passive to a scowl. The banging of drums came from behind him in the tent, but not like the harsh clashing of drum sticks in a band. It was the softer sound of hands tapping on skin drums.

'We wondered how long it would be before you came round. About the church fires, is it?'

'Yes. We're not here to accuse you, Mr...' He waited for the man to tell him his name, but when he didn't, he continued. 'Members of your group may have seen something, or heard something.'

The man peered suspiciously at Harrison, who had got out of the car to join them.

'Bring your back-up, did you? You know we're pacifists

here. We want to protect the environment, not burn down buildings or kill people.'

'Dr Harrison Lane,' Harrison introduced himself. 'Is that a drum circle I can hear?'

The man looked a little surprised. 'Yes. I'm a shamanic drummer.'

Harrison nodded and smiled. 'I enjoyed the powwow drums of my Native American stepfather and his community. Very soothing. The brain attaches to the rhythm and the sound vibrations help to increase the natural endorphins in the body. It's therapeutic. I sometimes use it for meditation.' Harrison said this more to DS Howard than the man, who he assumed already knew about its therapeutic benefits.

For the first time, the man smiled. 'Come on in, join us. We're almost done,' he said and waved Harrison forward.

DS Howard shrugged his shoulders to himself and followed in their wake.

Inside the large round tent structure were around twenty-five people, mixed genders and races, but all adults and dressed in similar bright handmade clothing as the man who had greeted them. They were sitting in a large circle around a big fire, which was piled high with logs and glowing red and white with heat. There was a strong smell of fresh wood smoke inside, which was slightly preferable to the stench of the church fires. All the people in the circle had a drum and were beating their hands on the skins in the same rhythm, their eyes closed. Their bodies swaying to the beat.

Harrison immediately found a space and sat in the circle on the floor with them, legs crossed. The man handed him a drum. Patrick, not wanting to be the only one left standing, followed his lead and found himself with a small wooden barrel type drum with a skin stretched over it. He watched what the others were doing and tried to follow their lead.

The rhythm of the group's drumming filled the yurt, and Patrick was surprised at how quickly his hands found the beat. Across the circle, Harrison smiled at him.

Patrick had forgotten about why he was there or just how furious his boss would be if she walked in right now and found him sitting on the floor with a bunch of drumming druids. He was surprised to find himself swaying to the beat with the group. It really was relaxing. When the drumming ended, he was almost disappointed.

The druid clapped his hands and once everyone had opened their eyes and focused, he introduced them to the group. They all smiled and said 'namaste'. Patrick almost felt bad about bringing up the topic they'd gone there to discuss.

'Thank you,' he said, looking around the group. 'We're investigating the murders of Reverend Soulsby and Davenport, and the burning of All Saints, St Luke's and St Mary's churches. Would any of you know anything at all about these? Have you heard anything or seen anything?'

The surrounding faces shook their heads.

'No strangers that you've not seen before?'

More head shakes.

'Nothing out of the ordinary at all?'

'There was the car fire last night,' a woman spoke up. 'I was out in the woods. Saw the flames and someone running away.'

'What time was this?' DS Howard asked.

'It was after we'd eaten, so between 6:30 and 7 p.m., I'd say.'

'Did you see the person?'

'Not their face.'

'What direction did they go?' Harrison asked.

'Towards the village.'

'How far would that be through the woods?'

'About fifteen minutes. It's an easy path.'

'Did you report the car fire?' DS Howard asked her now.

'No. We only have one mobile phone between us for emergencies. By the time I'd gone to check there was nobody inside and then started to head back, I heard a police car arriving. It would have been easy to see the car on fire from the road and it was in a clearing by a small lake, so little chance of the fire spreading.'

'Can you describe what the person had on? How tall they were?'

She shook her head. 'Not really. It was too far away and through the trees. But I think they had like a long black coat on. A thick one. It didn't flap around as they jogged. Maybe wool.'

DS Howard nodded. 'Were others with you?'

'We were all here besides Mari,' the man with the beaded beard explained.

'It was my turn to collect kindling,' Mari spoke up again, looking sheepish.

'In the dark?' Harrison queried.

Mari looked down into her lap, then threw a glance at the man. There was a pause.

He spoke for her. 'Mari had a disagreement with her partner. She went for a walk to clear the air. It happens. Everything is fine now. We've been honest with you. There's nothing to hide.'

'You complained about the church. Said they were brainwashing your children,' DS Howard challenged.

The fire came back into the man's eyes again.

'We wrote a letter to the school to ask them not to keep pushing Christian teachings onto our children. We have the right to refuse religious indoctrination, do we not? That does not make us murderers and pyromaniacs.'

'No,' DS Howard agreed.

He felt the mood of the group change and noted that they were very outnumbered, even with Harrison's fighting bulk.

'Well, thank you for your time. If you do hear or see anything that you think might be relevant to our inquiries, please get in touch. Whatever the religion, we have three dead men whose families need answers.'

Patrick got up from the floor, brushing down his trousers. Harrison rose with him. 'We'll see ourselves out. Thank you.'

They left the group, slipping through the tent flap and outside where snow whipped straight into their faces, melting instantly on their warm skin.

'That was a waste of time,' DS Howard said to Harrison as soon as they'd got into the car again.

'Maybe not,' Harrison replied. 'If her timings are right, then whoever set fire to that car could have come straight from the scrapyard, burned the vehicle to destroy evidence, and then returned to the village and the church fire, by the time the crowds had begun to thin out.'

'Or they could just have lived in the village and wanted to get rid of a car. It would have been cutting it fine. What they did to Reverend Davenport must have taken at least an hour.'

'Yes, but the fire brigade was there for around two and a half hours, plus the media circus arrived. People were coming and going. You didn't call me straight away and yet I was able to arrive and leave before everyone else had gone.'

'I wonder if any of the TV stations have footage we could look at. See if somebody was wearing a black coat.'

'And take a look at the body cams again. Was someone there at the beginning and end, but not for that crucial hour or two in the middle?'

'Yeah, you're right. Not sure that's going to keep the boss

happy, though. She's hoping I come back with a handcuffed druid.'

'It's not about her, it's about justice,' Harrison replied.

Patrick murmured a not very confident agreement and turned the car round to return along the bumpy track. It was easy for Dr Lane to say that, but not so easy for those like him who had to work under her. He wondered if Harrison felt as uncomfortable as him earlier, when the DCI had pocketed the theatre ticket at the crime scene. She'd only got away with it because the forensics officer was young and inexperienced. But he wasn't. He knew it was wrong. Question was, what could he do about it?

19

DECEMBER 19TH

Amelia Smith thoroughly enjoyed her job. For as long as she could remember, she'd wanted to work with the dead to help them tell their stories about what had happened to them. She could trace this passion back to when she was fourteen and a beloved uncle had been found dead in the street. Grief was tough enough for their family, but the long months trying to get answers to why he had died had a big impact on them all and cemented a career choice in the young Amelia's heart.

She did, however, work long hours with the pathologist, Dr Oliver Charles, or DOC as he liked to be called. When the morgue doorbell rang and she opened it to see a police detective and a man who introduced himself as Dr Harrison Lane, she made a vow to herself that she really needed to get out and socialise some more. Dr Lane was muscular and handsome and she couldn't help looking at his arms, which packed out the sleeves of the protective overalls she gave them, or his broad shoulders and tapered waist. She told herself that she was used to seeing naked bodies, and that's why she'd been so quick to mentally undress him the second he'd stepped into the lab; but in all honesty, she knew that was just an excuse. It was about time she got herself a boyfriend and she was unlikely to find one locked down here in the basement with the DOC and a fridge full of corpses, no matter how much she enjoyed her work.

The handsome Harrison Lane was a bit too old for her, although had he asked her for a date, she would have struggled not to say yes. For a few seconds she was thrown and had to give herself a mental shakedown before Dr Lane and the detective thought she'd lost the plot.

'Come on through here. We've got Martin Soulsby out ready for you, and DOC will be with you in five minutes. He's just finishing a procedure with Reverend Davenport.'

Amelia led the two men into a single examination room, depositing them and quickly exiting to find her boss before she embarrassed herself any further.

VISITING the druids had been a relaxing exercise thanks to their drumming, but coming to the morgue to see pathologist Dr Oliver Charles was never going to be such a pleasant event.

Harrison was glad that his clothes stank of wood smoke from the yurt, and even the church fires which had embedded themselves into the fibres of his jumper. The smell of a pathology lab was not something he wished to have in his nostrils. He could still smell the smoke even through the sleeve of the protective clothing the mortuary technician had just given them, so as not to contaminate the evidence from the bodies. He'd use it to fill his nostrils whenever the raw smell of the dead became too much.

The room, as in every morgue Harrison had been into,

was all steel units and white walls and floor. At its centre, a body in a white cadaver bag lay on top of a metal gurney on wheels. Everything else was steel. Instruments, sink, splash-backs. All gleaming and spotless to ensure no contamination. One of the ceiling light bulbs slightly flickered overhead, making it feel like standing in a horror movie set. Neither man said anything as they stared at the white body bag. They knew that what was in there wasn't going to be pleasant, but they also knew that it was a human being who deserved justice, and so they were going to have to just get on with it.

DS Howard jumped when the door suddenly flung open and the large frame of DOC bounded in, fully gowned up and wearing short white wellington boots. The blood splashes on his clothing and footwear were evidence of their necessity.

'Afternoon, gentlemen. Good of you to come and visit us. You have certainly presented me with two unusual cases. Most challenging. Beats the usual dose of weekend head injuries from the drunks, and organ failure thanks to over-doses. I'm not yet finalised with Reverend Davenport and I know the DCI wants the report ASAP, so shall we crack on with Martin Soulsby first?'

'Yes. Thank you, Dr Charles, please tell us all you can.'

'OK. I've got him on his front for you so you can see the back injuries. The poor fellow was cut to shreds.'

The pathologist unzipped the body bag carefully and peeled it back to reveal the white, putty-like flesh of Reverend Martin Soulsby's mortal remains. He hadn't been exaggerat-ing. The man's entire back was shredded. In some places it had cut so deep into the skin that it had almost exposed the bone.

'Bloody hell. What do you think caused this damage?' DS Howard asked.

Harrison could see the detective's eyes struggling to look at what was before them. In his own mind, all he could see was the collapsed shape of the man in the field being pecked by the crows.

'Nothing that you'd be able to buy over the counter. I think your perp made some kind of flagellation whip with razors along its length. He then beat him with it. I've managed to map out each strike. There was some damage from the crows, but it was minimal, thankfully. He was given forty lashes. That number becomes more significant later when we go and see Reverend Davenport.'

'Forty?' Harrison queried.

'Yes. Not forty less one.' DOC beamed at Harrison for knowing its significance.

Harrison saw DS Howard's nonplussed face and began to explain. 'Some people claim that Romans thought that forty lashes would kill a man. So, when punishment was meted out, they gave forty lashes less one in order to keep the victim alive for their suffering. It was also often a prelude to crucifixion under Roman law. They wanted them alive for that. It's claimed Jesus received thirty-nine lashes before being put on the cross.'

'So was this what killed Reverend Soulsby?' DS Howard asked DOC.

'In this case, I'd say not on its own. In those days the whips were leather, sometimes with added knots, and the punishment would have been meted out by a strong man chosen for the purpose. It's quite tiring whipping someone forty times. It would have also made quite a noise. Your killer relied on the razors to do the damage, so although I can see that some of the cuts were very deep, these were only the initial ones. Possibly initial anger or just that they started off with vigour, but as they tired, the cuts got shallower.'

'So what killed him?'

'He was forced to swallow a further forty razors, and then his mouth was gagged. He had them in his throat, oesophagus and mouth. His tongue and roof of his mouth were badly cut, his throat also. One sliced into the interior jugular vein. He lost a lot of blood. Then you add to this the fact he was in sub-zero temperatures dressed only in a thin shirt, and was clearly extremely shocked. The whole lot combined would have finished him off no problem. His heart failed, but I doubt he was conscious by then.'

'The razors, are they common, or do you think there's any chance we can trace them?'

'Gone off to Forensics, but I wouldn't hold out much hope there. They look like cheap razors you'd get from any chemists.'

'Would you be able to get any kind of handle on the time-frame all this took?' Harrison asked. 'I'm just trying to understand if the killer was torturing him to get information or some kind of confession out of him, or just to make him suffer?'

'That's incredibly hard for me to say, but...' The DOC narrowed his eyes, making the bags under them bunch up, and walked to the other side of Reverend Soulsby's remains. 'There are some indications of the skin on the back having started to bruise. You see here?' he said, bending down and indicating an area of skin.

Harrison and Patrick nodded, not wanting to prolong the inspection any longer than required.

'If you were asking me to stick my career on the line over this, I'd say he was whipped first, and then the razors were put into his mouth last. In which case, it's quite possible that it was torture to get information. But you understand that there are caveats to that and, of course, we've no idea what the killer's motive was.'

'Yes. Thank you.'

'There are no defensive wounds or any signs that he fought back,' the pathologist continued. 'It's as though he went willingly with his killer. He was forced to carry the wooden sheep he was found with. We've found paint and splinter evidence on both his shirt and the skin on his back.'

'Before or after the whipping?'

'Before. Some of the splinters had been embedded in the wounds. This whole spectacle took place in that field for sure. He'd been on his knees for some time in the mud and grass. Probably begging for his life too, poor chap.'

'It looked like at some point he leaned onto his killer as he walked across the field. Were any traces of a third party found on him or his clothing?' Harrison questioned.

'We have one. Just one black woollen fibre. It's not much to go on, I'm afraid, and also no guarantee that it's from your man.'

'Or woman,' DS Howard added. 'Could a woman have done this?'

'Physically? Absolutely. While the whipping did require some strength, they really dug those razors in deep. If she was fit, then there's no reason why a woman couldn't have done it.'

'And, Reverend Davenport, could a woman have killed him?'

The pathologist thought a moment, running through the wounds he'd just been logging in the room next door.

'Yes. Again, you're not looking at great strength involved. They used the magnet and crane to do the heavy lifting.'

'OK, thank you,' DS Howard replied quietly.

Harrison looked at the detective's face and wondered what was going through his mind.

'So, shall we move on to Edward Davenport?'

Both men nodded.

'This was something else again,' he said to them as they left Martin Soulsby behind and entered the next room. 'Quite an ingenious murder. I think I'm going to write this one up for our journal. Once the case is over, of course.' DOC looked to DS Howard and smiled.

They walked into a room which was identical to the one they'd just been in except that this room didn't have a flickering light, and was in mid examination. There were tools and various bits of equipment next to the fully uncovered remains of Reverend Edward Davenport, who was no longer as they'd seen him earlier. DOC had opened up his body, which now resembled a macabre red and white butterfly. At first, when Harrison looked, he couldn't make out what he was seeing.

'We scanned him. I'll show you the image later. As I said at the scene, he had been forced to swallow a large quantity of nails. Forty, to be exact.' The pathologist raised his eyebrows and looked at Harrison. 'He'd then been made to lie on his back and the magnet had drawn those nails forward through his flesh so that some of them protruded through his skin. You see the holes here on his stomach and chest? It would have been excruciatingly painful. If we turn him over, you will see the same marks on his back.

'He was then rolled over and picked up by the magnet on his back so that those nails were drawn in reverse through his body again and outwards. Finally, forty more nails were shoved into his mouth and throat and, again, a gag put over to make sure they stayed in.

'I'm not sure if he was still alive when he was hoisted up

for the final time, but my guess is that the final batch of nails were put in last and would have pierced his brain as the magnet pulled them up through the roof of his mouth and back palate, killing him pretty quickly if he wasn't already dead. I believe Dr Lane that you said at the scene that it was crucifixion from the inside out. And that's exactly what it was.'

'Didn't you say that the forty lashes were the prelude to crucifixion? So was this the second act? What can we expect next?' DS Howard asked Harrison.

'The resurrection.'

'Is that what the bishop has been taken for?'

'It could be. Maybe the killer is making the point that the bishop is risen from the dead to stand trial, just like the Cadaver Synod. They were definitely linking back to that with the chopping off of the Bishop's three right fingers.'

DS Howard let out a big sigh. 'Let's hope the dead bishop is his last act then. Anything else you can tell us about Reverend Davenport's final few hours, DOC?'

'Again, no defensive wounds. All indications are that these men either went willingly with their killer or were persuaded in some non-violent way. They could have had a gun pointing at them, of course.'

'You looked at Justin Black for us too, the verger who died at All Saints. Anything suspicious?'

DOC shook his head.

'Nothing that I could find and I went back and had another look after we brought in Reverend Soulsby, just to make sure he wasn't the first. His vital organs all showed the effects of extreme smoke, and his back was quite badly burnt where the ceiling had rained down on him. I believe it was an unfortunate accident.'

'Thanks, DOC.'

Harrison could see that DS Howard was itching to get out of the subterranean world of corpses and back out into the fresh air where their murderer still roamed alive.

'I'll have the Davenport report across to you in the next hour or so. Glad you boys came to me. Saves me having to face the dragon for at least the rest of today.' DOC winked and gave a cheeky grin.

Harrison could see that, despite the smiles, the man meant it. If senior staff like him didn't like the DCI's management style, then that didn't bode well for the rest of the team. He wondered what impact that might have on the investigation, and what lengths she would go to in order to get a conviction. He didn't have to wait long to find out.

20

DECEMBER 19TH

Ryan was cooking a lasagne in the microwave. He stood next to it, poised to turn it off before the loud ping sounded to announce it was ready. He'd already pulled the curtains shut and turned off all the lights. The room was now lit solely by the glow from his computer monitors and the temporary light from the microwave. He'd turned his phone to vibrate only, and put his computer on mute in case he accidentally clicked on a video that started playing automatically.

He could feel the tension in his neck and shoulders. It had even made him lose his appetite. His usual pile of daily snacks had sat untouched, and it was only because he had been feeling a bit lightheaded that he'd decided to put the lasagne in.

Addie had been up, knocking on the door several times already. Ryan had ignored him every time, but he knew he wasn't going to give up. If they knew he was definitely in, he might find the door wasn't as good a barrier to entry as he hoped.

He was already thinking through a plan B, should they break and enter. Last night, he'd slept on the sofa to make sure he heard any attempts to get through the door. Today, he'd rigged up cameras around the sitting room. If he pressed a certain button on his phone, they would start transmitting live to both Harrison and DS Jack Salter. Should Addie and his mates decide to kidnap him, then they'd know who they needed to find in order to track him down. If it went totally pear-shaped and they ended up killing him for doing a runner years ago, then he'd want to be damned sure that Jack and Harrison would be able to lock them up for it.

He'd also spent the afternoon creating home-made defences. A kitchen knife bound onto a wooden spoon, to give him more reach. A bottle of bleach decanted into a bottle of washing up liquid and slightly diluted so that it squirted out with force. He would not go down without a fight, even if it did mean ruining the rented flat's carpets. He'd worry about losing his deposit and having to pay for some new ones another time.

When he was positive that Addie had left the building, he fortified the door with some extra home-made locks. He'd had to improvise with what he had. His pride and joy was a bracket, straightened, and then screwed into the door frame and door. If he had a fire in the flat, he was going to get toasted. It would take him at least ten minutes to get out.

Ryan knew that he couldn't stay locked in the flat like this for long. He'd run out of food for one thing, and Addie was eventually bound to lose patience and smash the door down. Ryan just hoped that he could ignore them long enough for Harrison to come back to London. He'd sorted them out the first time. He'd know what to do.

His boss had called him for an update.

'Ryan, any news?'

It had been disappointing to tell him he'd found nothing so far.

'It's tough because we don't know what kind of time frame we're talking about.'

'I might be able to solve that one for you. Forty is significant to our killer. Now it could be something random, or it could mean forty years. Can you try all the possible uses of forty you can think of?'

'Sure.'

They'd chatted for a few more minutes about the evidence Harrison had seen and heard that day, and then his boss asked him how he was.

'You OK?'

'Yeah. Fine.'

'You're unusually quiet. I'm actually talking more than you are.'

Ryan cursed the fact the man missed nothing and not only knew him really well, but was an expert on human psychology.

'Just feeling a bit crap. I'll be fine.' It wasn't technically a lie. He did feel crap, but not because he was ill. He couldn't burden Harrison with this right now, not while he was away and in the middle of what sounded like an intense case.

'OK, if you feel up to it, can you check out a music concert for me? It's only a small local one, but I need to know if there's a list of seat numbers against names. I want to know who was in seat six, and, while you're at it, the complete list of who went.'

'No problem. I'll get onto it,' Ryan had replied, glad of the distraction. He'd waited for Harrison to send through the information and once he cooked his lasagne, spent the rest of the afternoon and evening tracking down the list of concertgoers.

He thought nothing more of it once he'd sent through the list of names to Harrison. Oblivious that it was to be a key piece of information.

21

DECEMBER 19TH

Harrison and DS Howard returned to the incident room, where it was immediately obvious the atmosphere had shifted.

'We've taken George Reid in for questioning. Found red diesel in his shed and a large quantity of nails,' a uniformed officer informed DS Howard as they walked in.

'The sexton?' Harrison asked him.

'Yep. Had keys for All Saints, and was there at all three crime scenes, so had plenty of opportunity.'

'It's his job,' Harrison replied, as much to DS Howard as to the other officer, who simply shrugged and moved on. 'Who will be interviewing him?'

'Possibly me. I've no doubt we'll find out soon enough.' DS Howard scanned the room. 'She's not here.' He looked at his phone to see if there were any messages. 'Let's grab a coffee quickly and see if there's been any other progress before she dishes out her orders.'

The refreshment area was an empty desk with a kettle and a stack of paper cups, along with a nearly empty box of tea bags, a jar of instant coffee and some milk. The surface was littered with little white plastic stirrers and countless sloshed beverage stains.

'You want one?' DS Howard asked Harrison.

'No, you're alright. I'll go and fill my water bottle.'

Harrison left the DS to his caffeine fix and went out to the reception area of the little police station, where he knew there was a water station.

He heard her before he saw her. She was laughing. The DCI was standing in the reception talking to a distinguished-looking man in a suit. He had the air of a person who knew his place in life and was confident in filling it. Harrison recognised him as one of the men the DCI had been talking to outside St Mary's. He looked to be in his mid to late fifties and was fortunate enough to have a full head of hair still, which was highlighted around the temples with grey. It didn't detract from his healthy good looks. Harrison could see from the DCI's body language that this was a man she was attracted to and comfortable around.

When Harrison walked into the reception, the DCI threw him a dirty glance and urged her companion forward and into the main building, smiling and thanking the officer on reception as she went through. Intrigued, Harrison quickly topped up his bottle and followed them. He was keen to find out who could make the DCI behave so charmingly.

When Harrison reached the incident room, they were nowhere to be seen. He retraced his steps, looking for them, but they'd gone.

'Who was that with the DCI?' he asked the officer at reception.

'That's the mayor, Lucas Fry. Came to offer extra resources or something.'

It wasn't unheard of, especially in a community like this,

but Harrison took out his phone and scrolled through the images he'd taken at the St Luke's scene when he'd arrived. There in the crowd of people was Lucas Fry, standing talking to an elderly couple. He had on a black woollen coat.

It wasn't evidence – there were others in the crowd in black coats. But Harrison logged it in his mind before returning to the incident room and rejoining DS Howard at his desk, where he was sipping tentatively at a brown sludgy liquid in a paper cup.

'I think you chose well.' The DS nodded at Harrison's water bottle.

'Tell me about the mayor,' Harrison asked.

Patrick did a double-take. 'The mayor? You mean Lucas Fry? Where's that one come from?'

'I've just seen him with the DCI. He was at St Luke's when I first got there, and again last night.'

'Yeah, well, that's not surprising. He is pretty good at being out and about in the community. A good bloke, really. One of those who actually listens to people, you know? Although I hear that the DCI has a bit of a thing for him. Poor geezer. The image of a female praying mantis biting off the head of her mate seems to come to my mind when I think of them.'

Harrison could empathise with Patrick's imagery. He was about to pull out his phone and show Patrick the photograph, but thought better of it. He'd no reason to suspect Lucas Fry other than the fact he was at St Luke's and St Mary's, and wore a black coat. Those were facts, but they weren't facts which would suggest that he was their killer. He'd need a lot more than that to accuse someone.

Before he could ask any more questions, the DCI marched into the room, heading straight for DS Howard.

'We've brought George Reid in for questioning. I've just

had confirmation that his DNA was found on Reverend Martin Soulsby's shirt. He's got red diesel and nails, and he has opportunity. I'm heading over to the custody suite now. I want you to join me.'

She didn't wait for an answer, and she didn't acknowledge Harrison. Instead, she marched off to the front of the room and picked up her bag and coat before exiting at the same speed. It was her coat which caught Harrison's eye. He'd not noticed it yesterday, but now that they were possibly looking for someone with a black woollen coat, he seemed to be seeing them everywhere. She had one flung over her arm.

'Well, I guess I've had my orders.' DS Howard sighed. 'Probably won't get a word in if she's leading the interrogation – I mean interview.'

'Mind if I come along? I met George at All Saints. He was the one who took me down to the crypt. I can honestly say that he didn't appear to have any prior knowledge that the bishop's body was missing. He looked genuinely upset.'

'Maybe he's a good liar. We'll see. But sure, you're welcome to sit next door. You won't be able to come into the room with us, though.'

THE DRIVE to the custody suite was a slower, more painful exercise than usual. The snow had started to settle and where it wasn't black slush, it was slippy. DS Howard had to concentrate hard to see through the endless blizzard of falling whiteness. The windscreen wipers were on full speed, but, every millisecond, the glass was plastered with more snowflakes.

It looked pretty. The afternoon had already turned dark with the sun hidden behind the grey snow clouds. With the time ticking away, the sparkling Christmas lights in people's windows created a festive scene that wouldn't have looked out of place on a Christmas card or a Hollywood movie set.

The two men drove in silence as the DS's need to concentrate meant he was unable to instigate conversation. Harrison looked out the window at children snow ball fighting in a park, and walkers, heads bent, their dogs wrapped in coats and looking miserable at the fact they'd been dragged out in the cold, wet weather.

When they arrived at the custody suite, they found DCI Lynne Turner sitting talking to a man in the reception. He wore a vicar's dog collar under a woollen jumper and an expression of fatigue and misery. He was shaking his head sadly.

'Reverend Galloway.' The DS put out his hand in greeting as he approached.

'DS Howard,' he returned the greeting. 'I was telling the DCI here that I can't believe George has been taken in for questioning. I can assure you there's no way that man would harm anyone.'

'We all like to believe the best in people, Reverend, but unfortunately we do have reason to ask Mr Reid some questions. He's not been charged or even arrested. He's just helping us with our inquiries at present,' the DCI answered for Patrick.

'Can I see him? As his spiritual counsel, if not as a friend?'

'Not just yet, but perhaps later.'

'Then I'll wait. The poor man doesn't have any family to support him. I'll not abandon him here alone.'

'Very well.'

The DCI motioned to DS Howard to follow her, ignoring Harrison, who had watched the scene play out. When she got up, he thought she'd pick up the black woollen coat next to her, but instead Reverend Galloway felt in the pocket of the coat for his phone and started to send a message to someone.

'He's a bit of a dramatist, isn't he?' the DCI whispered loudly to Patrick as they left the reception area. 'Might change his tune when he finds out that George has been dispatching his colleagues to their maker ahead of schedule.' Then she turned her head and looked at Harrison. 'Why are you here?'

'I'd like to listen in to the interview. See if George fits the profile that I've been developing.'

'It's not about profiles, Dr Lane, it's about hard graft and scientific proof. We have his DNA on at least one murder victim. We have red diesel, nitrile gloves, and nails found in his shed. He has access to all the crime scenes and I've been told that the new bishop was thinking about contracting out the upkeep of the churches and graveyards. Putting it out to tender. So we have a possible motive. Does that not count for anything in your world? While you're developing profiles, we're out finding a killer.' She said the words with vitriol and the look on her face hammered home just what she thought of him.

Harrison could have countered that all she'd mentioned was circumstantial evidence – if she had taken that to the Crown Prosecution service, they were unlikely to agree to George being charged. He didn't. Something he'd learned in his life, and particularly through his Taekwondo training, was that you chose your fights and you used your brain, not your ego or your anger. He wouldn't rise to the confronta-tional challenge. His time would come, but it wasn't then.

DS Howard shot him a sympathetic look, but Harrison's face remained unreadable. He needed to do some discreet digging about DCI Turner. Find out why she was so angry at him and pretty much most of the rest of the world. Had she always been like that? If so, how had she risen through the ranks? Was there another equally poisonous sponsor above her in the Force?

DS Howard deposited him in a small room that contained a viewing window into the next-door interview suite. The other side of it was mirrored and Harrison wondered if George would guess that somebody was behind its reflective surface, watching.

The DCI and DS Howard entered the room first. She chose her seat, and he sat in the one that was left. There was a slight agitation in her movements. A few repetitive traits that Harrison spotted and gave away she was building herself up to the interview. He doubted it was nerves; more like anticipation, perhaps even excitement. Like a cat preparing as it watched a bird. Twitching its muscles, ready to pounce.

George was followed in by a mouse of a man with brown hair and a sharp beak of a nose that dominated his face. It didn't bode well for the defence when he dropped his notebook, papers, and pen on the floor before he sat down. George helped him retrieve the items while the DCI looked on with disdain. The man's cheeks turned a bright red, making him look like a Christmas robin. Appropriate for the time of year, perhaps, but not the defence lawyer that George deserved.

The DCI didn't waste any time. She introduced herself and DS Howard and went through the necessary formalities, including turning on the recording. She asked George to state his name and confirm that he'd understood what she'd said.

George's voice was a ghost of its usual self, and she asked him to speak up. The man had little confidence at the best of times and Harrison could see that sitting, being stared at by two police detectives under the bright-white lights, was his worst nightmare. He'd tried to shrink down into the chair, pulling his disfigured face into his neck like a tortoise, but he and it had nowhere to go.

'We'd like you to tell us in your own words what you did on the sixteenth of December? Talk us through your day.'

'The sixteenth? Yesterday?' George looked from the DCI to his lawyer.

'No. The day of the All Saints fire.'

'All Saints. Yes. I wake up at 6 a.m. every morning. I had my breakfast. There was a funeral at St Mary's. I went to check the graveyard was tidy. Reverend Davenport had asked me to make sure the path was cleared. He was conducting the service. Sometimes small tree branches drop in the wind and the widow of the man who'd died was in a wheelchair. Reverend Davenport wanted to make sure she could get to the graveside easily. I picked up some twigs and there were a couple of bouquet wrappers that had been blown around.'

'Did anyone see you?' the DCI asked.

From next door, Harrison could see that the DCI was already getting agitated by the detailed description of George's day.

George shook his head.

'Can you answer yes or no for the benefit of the tape, Mr Reid?'

'No.' George looked even more uncomfortable.

Harrison understood his discomfort was because he purposely shunned company. He was a man who lived his life in the shadows as much as possible and avoided being seen.

'Where did you go after that?'

'I went to my store shed. Janice, one of the vergers at St Peter's, had asked me to look at the hinge on the gate. She said that kids had been swinging on it and people were having trouble closing it.'

The DCI seized the opportunity to question him about what was in his store shed.

'Do you have red diesel in your store shed, Mr Reid?'

'Yes, for the mower.' He looked from her to his lawyer again. 'I'm not using it illegally. We are allowed to have it. The council give it to us.'

'What about nails?'

'Nails?'

'Yes. Nails. You know, metal nails that you hammer into things.' Her tone was scathing, a bully trying to make him sound as though he was stupid.

'Yes. Of course. There are nails for fixing and building things. Screws too. I have lots of different things in the store shed.'

'Wire-cutters?'

'Yes.'

'Do you use nitrile gloves, George?'

'Nitrile gloves. I'm not sure'

'Latex gloves, the thin rubber ones you can throw away.' The DCI's mouth turned up on one side slightly as though she was half smiling.

Harrison recognised the expression for what it was. Contempt.

'Oh! Yes. I have to keep the rats and mice under control. We set traps for them and Reverend Galloway bought me a box. Said I shouldn't be touching the traps or the dead rats with my hands.'

'I see.' The DCI pressed her lips together and furrowed her forehead. She looked down at her lap for a few moments.

Harrison could see she was doing it for dramatic effect. She was psychologically pressurising him. George sat still and silent, waiting for her.

In interviews, Harrison watched every tiny movement

and gesture of body language. The tell-tale facial expressions that indicated someone was lying, or just the words that were used. George was nervous. A fish out of water. A man who hated scrutiny. But he wasn't a man who looked scared because he had something to hide. He was worried because of the situation he found himself in, but his face was open. There were no signs of him trying to keep nerves under control. No sweating. No struggling to put the right story together. What came out of his mouth was raw and immediate and full of detail. There were also no traits of psychopathy that could explain the level of control that could achieve that effect without it being true. In short, George was innocent.

'Could you tell me how your DNA got onto the shirt of Reverend Soulsby? The shirt he was wearing when he was found brutally murdered in the fields near to St Luke's?'

George's mouth dropped open. 'Shirt? DNA?'

DS Howard had sat silent up to this point, his boss totally dominating the interview. Harrison could see him look at the DCI, who showed no signs of enlightening George any further. She was enjoying seeing him struggle with the questions. Wallowing in what she saw as her superiority and his ignorance.

'The shepherd's long shirt that the Reverend Soulsby was wearing in the nativity play. Your unique genetic fingerprint was found on the shirt, which indicates that you'd been in contact with it,' DS Howard explained to George.

'His nativity tunic,' George replied, the relief washing across his face. 'Yes, the vicar asked me to bring the tunic and the sheep, and all the other costumes and props out of storage for the dress rehearsal. We use the same ones each year. Sometimes I have to do some repairs or Mrs Linley, who does the flowers, mends the costumes – you know, if a moth has got to them over summer or something.'

The DCI's cheek twitched. 'Where were you between the hours of 5 p.m. and 11 p.m. on the night of the St Luke's fire?'

'The night after All Saints? I was at home. It had been a hard day. I'd been helping the firemen and police at All Saints; it was very upsetting.'

'Can anyone verify that you were home?'

George thought for a few moments and shook his head. 'I live on my own. Maybe my neighbour, but I'm not sure.'

'What about the day after? You helped with the boxing up and removal of items from St Luke's and All Saints, to be stored at St Mary's, is that right?'

'Yes. Reverend Galloway thought it would be a good idea to take them away from the damaged buildings and store them where we could lock them up to keep safe.'

'We found a small bottle of sulphuric acid in your work-room. Why would you have that?'

The change of direction in questions made George's eyebrows come together. Harrison knew where she was going.

'I've never needed to use it. I think it was for the drains. We need to keep the drains and soakaways clean. That sulphuric acid has been there since before my time. They used to dilute it and put it down the drains. I kept it in case we needed it – don't like to throw anything away. It's safely stored.'

'So you didn't use it to create the incendiary device?'

'Incendiary device?' George looked from the DCI to his lawyer, questioning.

'The device that caused the small explosion and fire at St Mary's.' The DCI spelled it out for him with disdain.

George looked horrified. 'No. No, why would I do that?'

'Do you enjoy your job, Mr Reid?'

'Yes.'

'And how long have you been doing it?'

'Since I was seventeen. I started as the assistant to the sexton and now it's just me.'

'Am I right that the new bishop is considering putting the jobs of maintaining the graveyards and the buildings out to tender with local contractors?'

George's eyes saddened. 'He wrote to me, said it was something they might do.'

'And how did that make you feel?'

He didn't answer immediately. George hung his head and looked down, his brow flattening. Harrison could hear him breathe in several times, an indication of the sadness he was feeling. He searched for words to describe emotions he'd never discussed before.

'Sad.' Was his only reply.

'Sad. Not angry perhaps? Angry enough to want to destroy them?'

George looked up, animated. 'No. No. Never. It's terrible what has happened,' he almost shouted at her. The first time they'd heard his volume rise. 'Those churches have been there centuries. They're like friends to me. I'd never damage them.'

'What about the vicars?'

'The vicars? What are you trying to say?'

Harrison was getting increasingly agitated by George's discomfort, and even DS Howard shuffled in his chair. He knew that everyone had to be looked at and considered during an inquiry. That those with opportunity should be questioned so they could be eliminated from it, but this wasn't the DCI's motive here. She was clearly trying to push the blame onto the sexton. He could be an easy scapegoat. If she had somebody in the frame, then it would take the pressure off her.

George's lawyer seemed to finally wake up and realise he was there to represent his client's best interests – and that things were getting out of hand.

'I think that's enough questions for my client. He strongly denies any connection to the crimes that you're investigating and he has cooperated fully with your inquiry. If you aren't going to charge him, then I believe we are done.'

DCI Turner's face hardened. 'That is all for now. Thank you. But, Mr Reid, we are continuing our investigations and so I would appreciate it if you could ensure you are available if we have any further questions. We will be cross-checking and verifying what you have said to us today and will be back in contact.'

With that, she terminated the interview and recording and flounced out of the room.

George looked shellshocked. 'I didn't do anything. Why does she think I would do that?' he asked his solicitor and DS Howard.

'We have to ask some difficult questions as part of an investigation like this. If you're innocent, then there's nothing to fear,' the DS replied. 'Reverend Galloway is in the reception waiting for you. I'll take you through.'

George's shoulders immediately softened at the vicar's name. He followed DS Howard out of the interview room, eager for a friendly face.

Harrison followed them. The interview had resulted in no new information. He was less than impressed with the DCI's cross-examination skills. The one thing it had achieved was to confirm to him that George was definitely not their killer. It had also raised more questions in his mind as to why the DCI was so keen to prove that he had.

22

—

DECEMBER 19TH

Three hours later, at a packed media conference, it wasn't immediately clear that DCI Turner believed in George's innocence. She was standing on the small village hall stage, the wife of Reverend Soulsby sitting on her left, and Reverend Galloway on her right. Mrs Soulsby had given a heart-wrenching plea to whoever had killed her husband, or to anyone who might know anything, to come forward. The family of Edward Davenport were absent. Too traumatised to face anyone. The police were still battling to get photographs of Reverend Davenport's body hanging from the crane deleted from various social media sites, but it was a losing battle. It had spread globally across all the social media platforms frequented by the human vultures.

'I can assure you that we are making progress with the inquiry. We have DNA and a person of interest and we are conducting further investigations,' DCI Turner was saying to the room.

Harrison was standing at the back, watching. He'd looked on incredulously as she'd played the part of the empathetic detective with Mrs Soulsby. When the DCI had held her hand, Soulsby's widow broke down. It had made his skin crawl.

The DCI also told a good lie, unless she really believed that George was their killer. In which case, she was a terrible detective.

'Have you arrested anyone?' a journalist spoke up from the seats.

'Not yet. As I said, this is an ongoing investigation and we have a person of interest identified.'

'Is it true that you've taken George Reid, the man who looks after all the church buildings and graveyards, in for questioning?'

'Mr Reid was helping us with our inquiries. He hasn't been arrested.'

Harrison bristled at her reply. She should have been more forceful with rebutting that question. It could lay George open to abuse. In situations like this, when emotions were running high, vigilantism could easily spark up, and that was when potentially innocent lives could get ruined. The interview with him had effectively debunked all DCI Turner's circumstantial evidence – unless he was a master of deception, which Harrison highly doubted.

'Reverend Galloway, are you concerned, scared?' Another question from the audience.

DCI Turner looked at him and sat down, allowing him to speak.

'I am deeply concerned about the motivations of the individual or individuals who have been conducting these terrible crimes. We have lost three wonderful people from our community and I've lost three dear colleagues. Two who were brutally murdered and a third who died trying to save his beloved church. I urge whoever is behind this to come forward and to seek forgiveness. My door is always open to anyone who is struggling. I will never turn away from anyone and I will never be frightened into giving up my work. The devil will not prevail. Our community will work together to find a way forward.'

'Is it true that pagans could be to blame? Didn't you find some kind of ancient pottery figures at each crime scene? Could this be anti-Christian terrorism linked to the winter solstice?' A reporter in the front row asked anyone on the stage who would answer.

'Let's not use inflammatory language,' DCI Turner said, taking over from Reverend Galloway.

Harrison could see that as soon as the words had left her lips, she regretted it. Inflammatory was an unfortunate choice of words.

'We have no evidence to suggest this is an organised group targeting the Church establishment. And that's all the questions we have time for. We need to get back to work.'

As the DCI ended the press conference, a surge of journalists clamoured forward to ask for interviews. The story was selling papers and leading news bulletins.

She stood up again and shouted, 'There will be no more interviews for today. Please put your requests in to our media liaison.'

Harrison left the squabbling behind and walked back through the snow to the incident room. The noise behind him was like a shed full of turkeys, all trying to have their voices heard above the din. Outside, the snow had brought a kind of peace. The noise of everyday life muffled by a soft layer of white cotton wool.

Everywhere was covered in snow. The roads still retained the tracks of tyres, but once night fell and the vehicles were off the road, this would freeze over and be covered by more snow. By the morning, it was going to be increasingly difficult to get about. Harrison hoped he wasn't going to get stuck here for Christmas. For the first time in his life, he had a reason to be somewhere.

Back at the incident room, a tired-looking DS Howard was hunkered over his keyboard. When Harrison sat down next to him, the DS looked at him with red eyes.

'You fancy some pizza? We've got a mountain of it on order. Just hoping it's not cold by the time it gets here through the snow.'

'No thanks. I need to do some exercise first. Thought I'd head back to my hotel room.'

'You know there's a gym next door, right? Well. When I say a gym, I might be slightly overstating it. There's a room with exercise equipment. They've got treadmills, free weights, a rowing machine and a few other bits of equipment in there. The superintendent insisted on it being set up because everyone was getting lazy and fat. Don't think it's been used that much.'

'Thanks. Might be preferable to a gym full of hung-over partygoers. I've got my running kit in the car. Had hoped the snow warnings would be wrong. I'll give it a go.'

'Pop back for some pizza if you want afterwards. But can't promise there'll be any left. It tends to be more popular than the gym round here.'

Harrison waved a thanks as he left the incident room to get his kit. He doubted he'd be able to swallow a mouthful of pizza if he had to do it in the same room as the DCI.

HARRISON LIKED TO EXERCISE, but when he was frustrated and angry, he needed it. Sitting and watching DCI Turner interview George today had wound him up. She knew the man wasn't particularly well educated or intelligent, and she'd used that to her advantage. Bullying him had clearly given her pleasure, and he was extremely worried that should her job or reputation be on the line, she wouldn't hesitate in trying to use him as a scapegoat.

There were always some bad apples in any barrel. He'd met a few of them in the Met. Usually, their reputations went before them and he knew how to keep out of their firing line, but one thing he wouldn't stand for was to see somebody like George, who was alone and vulnerable, being bullied. He needed to run out the anger which coursed through his veins.

Harrison collected his kit bag from the boot of his hire car. There was a good inch of snow all over the vehicle, but at least it was fine and powdery, so it would be easy to clear off later. As he was heading back into the building, his mobile rang. DI Seb Bartholomew from the National Crime Agency.

'Harrison, how's it going down there? Just seen the press conference on TV. There's no real mention of it being a ritualistic crime, so if I've sent you there on false pretences, don't feel like you have to stay. Head home.'

'No, it's fine. There is a definite religious element to the crimes. The killer is using various metaphors and symbolism in what he's doing, but I believe it's a personal vendetta that's behind this.'

'What does DCI Turner think?'

Harrison paused a moment to think how to word his response.

'She hasn't welcomed my input.'

'Oh crap, apologies. I'm not surprised. Didn't know it was going to be her running things when we first got the request in from Detective Superintendent Mark Ferry. We've got a bit of history with Lynne Turner.'

'History?'

'Yeah. She has tried several times to join the NCA, but never successfully. There's always some alarm bell that goes off. I've not met her. What's she like?'

'Forceful. Doesn't listen to anyone else. Has zero leadership skills and is downright rude a lot of the time.'

'Nice! A real team player. Sounds like we made the right choice then. Look, like I said, if you don't feel you're adding value then don't be afraid to just cut your losses and head home. I'm aware you're not supposed to be on the job yet, anyway.'

'I'll stick around for a bit longer,' Harrison replied. There was no way he was going to leave just yet. He didn't trust DCI Turner to ensure justice was done and there were victims and their families who deserved that, not to mention George who needed protection.

'OK. Well, let me know how it goes or if you need anything. Enjoy the winter wonderland. My kids are loving the snow. Been a while.'

DS HOWARD HAD BEEN RIGHT. The 'gym' consisted of a somewhat narrow, cold room with a thin grey carpet, no windows, and a few pieces of equipment in it. It looked like it had probably once been a storeroom or locker room. Either way, it would have to do for now. He just wanted to get on the treadmill and run.

Harrison warmed up and then did a few free weights before getting onto the treadmill. Slowly, he built up the speed, finding his breathing and feeling the muscles in his legs and buttocks warm up. His heart rate began to rise as he steadily increased the speed, enjoying the rhythmic thump of his feet and the whirr of the treadmill.

Harrison tried to empty his mind of the day's events, to

rid himself of the tension which resulted from anger. He wanted his muscles to be relaxed and ready, not tight and hard. It should be his brain which focused on the case, not his emotions. He rolled his shoulders and shook out his arms.

As he upped the speed higher, his body began to complain at the extra work. His back broke out in a sweat, and he relished the feeling of pushing every muscle, every sinew harder. He felt his abdominal muscles working with his lungs. Pumping the breath in and out. He increased the speed further.

It was at some point during the flat-out running stage that he felt a change in the room. It was hard to describe the feeling, but he sensed that somebody had come in and was now stood watching him. His back was to the door and there was no mirror to look behind him. He couldn't turn round because that risked him losing balance at this speed and falling. Yet it felt like the hairs on the back of his neck had risen in response to a threat.

Then he saw her. Her shadow was reflected in the computer screen of the treadmill. A dark outline of a tall woman standing with arms crossed and leaning against the door frame. DCI Turner.

He knew she was watching him, but he didn't want to stop running immediately and give her the satisfaction of knowing she'd interrupted him. So he ran for another minute or so. Pushing himself to stay focused on his body. It was no good. He realised that it would be impossible to reach the usual peaks of his stamina when all he wanted to do was turn around and challenge her. His body wanted to fight her, not run. He slowed the speed back down to a jog and then a walk and got ready for the confrontation ahead.

23

DECEMBER 19TH

DCI Turner couldn't help but be impressed by the muscular man in front of her on the treadmill. His shoulders rippled through the thin white T-shirt he wore. It clung to his skin with the sweat that left damp patches in a T shape down his back. He was certainly fit. The thought of running her hands over that body, feeling his solid thighs and biceps, was very appealing. But she and Harrison Lane were never likely to be bedfellows.

She waited for him to get tired. Thinking about the blood pumping through his body. The heat from his skin. The testosterone coursing around his muscles. Finally, he slowed the treadmill down. His back heaving with the effort of his lungs. He'd be surprised to see her when he turned round. Perhaps embarrassed. She'd enjoy taking the upper physical ground.

Harrison stopped and bent forwards with his hands on his knees, stretching his calf muscles. His shorts rode up slightly, giving her a tiny, teasing peek of his lower buttocks.

She allowed herself the pleasure, sure in the knowledge that he couldn't see where her eyes were resting.

'DCI Turner,' he said, without turning around. 'Is there something I can do for you?'

She almost jumped in shock. She'd been expecting to surprise him. How the hell did he know she was there? Quickly, she regained her composure.

'I want to have a word with you in relation to some of the questions that came up at the press conference.'

Harrison finally turned around, still on the treadmill, and wiped the sweat from his forehead with his arm. 'OK.'

'Have you been talking to the press about your theories? Why is it that the question of the winter solstice and pagan figurines came up? That could only have been because somebody has been talking to the media.' She'd said it with as much authority as she could muster because, try as she could, he'd unbalanced her.

'Not me. I've no idea. I don't talk to the media.'

'You expect me to believe that?'

'You can believe what you like, DCI Turner, but you asked me a question and I've given you the answer.'

She narrowed her eyes and stared straight into his as he stepped down from the treadmill.

'I know all about you, Dr Lane. I know what you're from. A psychopathic serial killer as a father and a mother who died by suicide. Not a great gene bank to come from, is it? Your puerile attempts to prove your mother's death was murder will fail. You're being watched.'

As she'd spoken, Harrison had slowly walked up to her. He'd seemed to grow in size with every word that she uttered. Intimidating didn't do the effect justice. He stood directly in front of her face, his eyes burning into her skull. She could feel the heat coming off him. See the veins pulsing in his neck and his swollen muscles. One more step and they'd be nose to nose. If she pushed him just a little further, maybe he'd snap. She could get him suspended. Arrested for assault.

'Still the mummy's boy, aren't you?' she tried. Her own body was rigid with tension and the expectation of retaliation. It wouldn't be the first time a man had hit her. She knew too well that it hurt.

Harrison edged closer, his jaw tight, cheek twitching with anger. She could smell him. The hot, fresh sweat of a man who was ready to fight.

Then he smiled.

'You're correct, DCI Turner.' His voice was soft, deep, and calm. 'My childhood was a little unusual, but I'm pleased to hear that I'm being watched because that can only mean one thing. That I'm on the right track.

'Clearly you feel threatened by me. I can see how shallow your breathing is, and the minute expressions of fear on your face that you're trying to disguise under that smug exterior. But why be afraid of me? Unless, that is, you're not a good police detective and there's something far more important you're trying to hide?'

'Is that a threat, an accusation?' she snapped back, completely thrown by his cool response and unable to think of anything else.

'A threat? I've not threatened you. I'm here to assist your inquiry. As I've said to you before, I deal only in facts. That was a statement of fact based on the body language you're displaying. Have a good evening, DCI Turner. The gym is all yours. There's a punch bag over there in the corner. You might like to give that a try.'

He walked past her, his eyes not leaving hers. Their bodies just centimetres from touching. For a moment she thought about pushing into him, trying to goad him further.

Elicit some kind of physical contact so that she could scream and call for help, but he was gone before her body, frozen on the spot, could act. He picked up his bag and left, without another word or look.

DCI Lynne Turner realised he'd been right. Her breathing was fast and shallow in her chest. The second she was alone, she gulped in big breaths, gasping at the air for a few moments as she tried to calm down from the encounter.

He was intimidating physically and mentally. He was very dangerous. She could see why some in the network thought he was a serious threat. They'd have to do a lot more than send one female DCI to deal with him. They were going to need a small army and a lot of influence to end Dr Harrison Lane's career and prevent him from finding out the truth. She took her phone from her pocket and dialled the number she'd been given to report back.

24

DECEMBER 19TH

Harrison was reeling. He'd thought she was just a local bully, but what DCI Lynne Turner had just said to him suggested that she wasn't alone. There were others who were out to get him, or to at least stop him from finding out the truth about his mother's death. How? Who?

Perhaps Desmond Manning's arrest had set the warning bells going and alerted them to the fact he was coming for them. No doubt Desmond wouldn't hold his tongue. The little weasel would have blabbed to someone. Anyone. Was it the same people who had murdered his mother and covered up her death all those years ago? Why should it matter now to anyone else, unless there was a need to protect someone very high up?

He had so many questions still to answer, but, as always, he needed to put his own personal crusade aside and concentrate on helping the victims of crime who were unable to help themselves, and to prevent any further deaths.

Harrison had quickly got changed, ready to head out into

the snow to go back to the hotel. He was so lost in thought that he nearly walked into Reverend Galloway, who was rushing into the small police station reception area as he was walking out.

'My apologies,' the vicar said, even though it was more Harrison's fault than Galloway's. 'You were with DCI Turner earlier, weren't you? Would it be possible to see her? I'm extremely concerned about the safety of George Reid.'

Harrison looked at the man. Most people in his shoes would have been more concerned about their own safety after recent events.

'Is he in imminent danger?' Harrison asked.

'I don't know. A parishioner has told me that she heard a group of men saying they were going to go round to his house to talk to him. One of them was the cousin of Martin Soulsby and they've been in the pub so are fuelled with alcohol. I'm afraid that they want to do more than just talk and George will be terrified. He struggles to socialise, let alone deal with conflict like that.'

'I'll go round there now and check he's alright. Talk to DS Howard. He'll be able to help you. The DCI has other concerns right now.'

Reverend Galloway nodded and crossed to the reception desk. Harrison texted the DS to warn him. He didn't want the DCI coming through reception and spotting the vicar. There was no way she'd be interested in protecting George Reid.

Patrick confirmed he'd be straight out. Harrison was long gone before he got there.

GEORGE REID's home came with his job. A small workman's cottage with the store shed and workshop needed to maintain the churches, attached. It was not a home for a family. In truth, it wasn't much of a cottage. There was just one bedroom and a living room. Even an estate agent's clever lenses and camera angles would have struggled to make the rooms look spacious. A cat would have been safe from any swinging in this house. It was, however, more than enough for George to call it home.

It was located down a little lane around a hundred yards from St Peter's, Reverend Frank Galloway's church. George's only neighbour was an eighty-five-year-old widow who had a small modern bungalow on the corner of his lane. Unfortunately, Mrs Melrose was deaf and had mobility issues. She hadn't heard the two cars which drove up and disgorged seven agitated men outside George's home.

By the time Harrison arrived, the men were banging on George's front door and shouting for him to come out. Two of them were laughing as they pulled apart his Christmas wreath, which they'd ripped from the door, and were scattering green and red across the white snow, an intimidating foretelling of their intentions.

Harrison jumped straight out of his car and marched down the path towards them. He could hear talk of stones and breaking windows if George didn't appear.

'What are you doing?' he shouted. 'Go home now and don't come back or I'll call the police and have every one of you arrested.'

The man who was clearly the ringleader puffed out his chest and pushed himself forward in the group. 'It's him who should be arrested. Who the hell are you telling us what to do?'

'You reckon you could take on seven of us, do ya, big fella?'

'I believe that I could, yes. I also don't want to have to hurt anyone. So I am going to ask you again to turn around and leave. Now.'

The man muttered some expletives to his friends.

While they postulated, Harrison was assessing the situation. The ringleader was the biggest of them, but he was overweight and no doubt slow. He was also clearly inebriated, and so his coordination would be shot. There were two other slightly younger men who looked like they'd be able to stand up for themselves in a fight, but the rest of them were now huddled like frightened chickens behind them. Harrison very much doubted that any of them had anywhere near the combat training that he'd had, or the stomach to take him on.

Harrison also assessed the terrain. The path was covered in snow and fairly slippery. To his left was a small fence behind which there were some low-level bushes and then what was probably a lawn, although he couldn't see due to the snow coverage. On his right was an open area that led to the workshop and store shed. Again, he couldn't see the ground, but he suspected this might be concrete or tarmac. It would be easy for them to walk away across that area, where he could see their cars parked up along the lane. Harrison was standing at the bottom of the path, facing them. They had their backs to the cottage. The position he ideally needed to be in was up against the front door where he could use it, and the porch above it, to his advantage. He'd have to make do.

Before he allowed himself the pleasure of getting rid of the pent-up anger from his discussion with the DCI, Harrison tried a more diplomatic tack.

'You do realise that Mr Reid has not been charged with any crimes? That he has dedicated his life to looking after the churches and their grounds. He is not the man who murdered Reverend Soulsby nor Davenport. Nor is he the man who set fire to the churches.'

'Who the hell are you? You're not from round here. What do you know?' the ringleader snarled again. 'Maybe it's you we should be after.'

'You can by all means try, but my name is Dr Harrison Lane. I'm head of the Ritualistic Behavioural Crime Unit with the National Crime Agency. I'm here to help the police find out who did commit these crimes.'

'You don't look like a copper?' another man said now, looking him up and down.

'I'm not a police officer. I'm a psychologist.'

'A bloody shrink here to look after the freak,' the ringleader blabbered.

'I said psychologist, not psychiatrist. Perhaps if you had a little more intelligence, both cerebrally and emotionally, you wouldn't make statements like that about other people. I don't know Mr Reid well, but he is certainly a far nicer human being than you appear to be.'

Harrison was ready for it. The man let rip with a string of expletives and ran straight at him, fist raised.

One restrained punch to his chin was enough to send him reeling backwards into the arms of his friends. He shook himself like a winded terrier.

'You're welcome to try that again,' Harrison growled. 'Or as I've suggested, you can walk back to your cars and never return.'

'Come on, lads, let's beat the bastard,' the ringleader shouted, calling on the men behind him. Four of them heeded his call, including the two younger men. Two of the group didn't move at all, but watched the scene play out in front of them with their mouths open. They were probably the more sober in the group, and Harrison imagined would have driven the cars.

Harrison used the slippery path to his advantage. He jumped out of the way of the ringleader, who then slid along the path, unable to stop his momentum. It allowed him to deal with the next two men, who were closing in together like a pair of bulldogs. A couple of well-targeted swinging kicks took the legs out from under the first, and, as he went down, the other was forced to swerve to avoid him. Taking advantage of his upset balance, Harrison gave him a big shove so that he tipped backwards over the fence, into the low bush, and summersaulted backwards onto the lawn. By this time, the other two men had already assessed their chances and decided the best move was to head off across the yard area to the cars, following in the snowy imprints of the two who had already made that decision.

Harrison turned just as the ringleader came back for his next attempt, desperately swinging a punch. Harrison ducked, but the fist still made contact, just glancing off the side of his head. Anger shot through him. The anger he'd tried hard to dissipate by running in the gym but which had been made worse by his altercation with the DCI. Now he was faced with a coward of a man who was trying to bully someone weaker than him. A victim who was innocent and frightened.

The switch was flicked.

Harrison's only focus was to thrash the low-life in front of him. There was no more playing nice.

He hooked his leg around the man's and half knocked him and half spun him to the floor in seconds. There was a loud thud and groan as the man hit the floor and had the wind forced out of his lungs. Before Harrison could launch a first punch, a voice came from behind him. Harrison swung round instinctively to defend himself.

'You might need these.' It was DS Patrick Howard, closely followed by a uniformed police constable and the vicar. The DS held out a set of handcuffs and had his eyebrows raised, alarm on his face. A warning that Harrison should use the handcuffs and not his fist.

It took him a few moments, but Harrison's awareness returned. He dropped his arm and tried to bring his breathing under control. Forcing the anger from his brain first, and then out of his body. He took the cuffs and secured the man's hands. His prisoner was still writhing and shouting expletives, but he was going nowhere now.

'I'll take over,' the DS said to Harrison. 'Dougie Soulsby, I am arresting you for assault and no doubt several other charges to do with attempting to threaten a member of the public and causing an affray.'

Dougie swore again. 'Get this big bastard away from me, would you?'

Harrison stepped back, not to appease Dougie, but to make DS Howard's job easier, and looked to see where the others had gone. The uniformed police officer was talking to the other four men who had stayed for the fight, and were now standing in a huddle, two of them covered in snow and looking very sheepish. The cars and the other two were nowhere to be seen.

Reverend Galloway stepped forward, avoiding the prone Dougie, and went to knock on George's front door.

'George, it's Reverend Galloway – Frank. Are you alright? Can you open the door for me? The police are here. Everything is OK now.'

Once DS Howard had read Dougie Soulsby his rights, he

left him to the uniformed police officers who had arrived with a van to cart him off to the custody suite.

'You OK? I saw him punch you,' he said to Harrison.

'Yeah, fine, just glanced me. I hope George is alright.'

'The vicar will talk to him. We'll set something up in case this happens again, but to be honest, with Dougie banged up I don't think we need to worry too much. The guy's always been a troublemaker. I was just talking to Reverend Galloway when a call came in. George's neighbour, Mrs Melrose, was on her way to bed and looked out the window to see a group of men outside his cottage. We came over straight away, but looks like it was a good job you got here before us.'

Harrison said nothing. He knew it was also a good job that the DS arrived when he did, otherwise Dougie might well be needing an ambulance. He'd had every intention of beating the man to a pulp. There had been so much anger coursing through his body, he'd been like a mouse trap ready to snap. Exactly the outcome that would have made DCI Turner smile and have proved her right about his genetic heritage.

He was disappointed in himself.

'See you tomorrow,' he said.

'Sure. They'll need a statement from you.' DS Howard indicated his uniformed colleagues, who were bundling the men into the custody van.

Harrison just nodded and left. They knew where to find him. He needed to close the door in his hotel room and be alone for a while. As he walked away, the anger starting to leave him, Harrison realised that while being on his own would get rid of irritations like Dougie Soulsby and the DCI, he could never escape himself and who he was.

25

DECEMBER 19TH

The press conference had been interesting. The media really were totally clueless if they believed that someone like George Reid could commit such finely planned acts. But then again, so were a lot of people. George wouldn't have to suffer for long. He was an accidental victim of this game plan.

Just one more day and it would be the grand finale. A time to reveal all and claim the ultimate victim. The man who had started this whole chain of events off, forty years ago, would finally get what he deserved.

The headaches were bad today. It was hard to concentrate when your whole head screamed and throbbed. It made the anger easier, though. There was plenty of that.

Twenty-four hours and the suffering would be over.

26

DECEMBER 19TH

It had been a long time since Harrison had allowed the anger to take control of him, but it was always there, just like DCI Turner had said. A poison in his blood, passed down from a father he never even knew.

One more slip up like that and his career with the NCA could be over. He'd be OK, but he wouldn't be able to help the victims who needed him.

DS Howard had averted a crisis, but he hadn't emptied the dam of anger that bubbled inside Harrison.

The minute he was back in his hotel room, he locked the door and flung himself onto the bed. Exhausted. So much emotional angst in his own life, let alone the pressure of an investigation and a senior police officer who was out to see him fail.

Harrison could feel the tension in every one of his muscles. He got off the bed and sat cross-legged on the floor. When the need was this bad, he had to do some kind of movement to help him meditate. Just lying still and imagining each muscle relaxing wouldn't help. His mind was whirring.

He closed his eyes and threaded his fingers together, like a church steeple, connecting. Then he breathed in, slowly and deeply, squeezing his hands together before releasing them and stretching his arms out to the sides, opening his chest and diaphragm so that he could breathe as deeply as possible. Then, he slowly let the breath out, bringing his arms back together and interlacing his hands once more. He repeated it, time after time. Finding his own natural breathing rhythm and concentrating on making the movements fluid. Effortless. Focusing his mind totally on the feeling of his hands gripping each other and floating through the air, before returning to connect.

Slowly, the vivid red anger of the day subsided. He pushed thoughts of DCI Turner, the incident at George's house, and the question of who the killer was, out of his mind. He was just here. In this moment. Breathing.

Finally, when he at last felt calm, Harrison got up from the floor and filled up the little kettle to make tea. He wasn't someone who suffered from the cold, but as he always turned the heating in hotel rooms down to the minimum, he was beginning to feel the chill. He realised his trousers bottoms were damp from the snow, but suspected that Dougie was an awful lot wetter and hoped he was cold and miserable, or sitting in custody-issued trousers and a top that stripped away his dignity.

He felt a bubble of anger again and pushed it away. He had to turn this into positive energy.

Harrison hadn't checked his phone for a while, so after ordering some room service dinner, he sat down to look through his messages. There was an email from Ryan.

Managed to get the list of ticket sales for the concert. There are a few photos on social from the event too, so we can verify if the person who bought the ticket was there or not.

Harrison clicked on the attachment and brought up a list of over a hundred names with numbers. He knew exactly what number he was looking for. Front row, number six. If the DCI had been telling the truth, then her name would be against it.

It wasn't.

Harrison's heart gave a little jump. Could this be their first solid clue? Or perhaps the original seat buyer had been unable to attend and had given her the ticket? He scrolled through the images that Ryan had sent. There was no mistaking them. She was tall and blonde and sitting in the row behind. He had a full head of dark hair, streaked with grey and framed at the temples.

She'd lied. He scanned the list again and saw her name. She was in the seat she'd bought. One row back, seat twelve. He went back to the photograph. There was no disputing it.

So had she been mistaken? Assumed that it was her ticket without taking in the number? He thought back to that moment. The flicker that went across her face and the way she quickly snatched the ticket and pocketed it to avoid any further view of it. Was she working with him? He'd been there today. Was she trying to get the murders blamed on George in order to save him?

What was her story? Her anger had to be more than just having been turned down a few times by the NCA.

Harrison was straight on the phone to Ryan.

'Good job with the tickets, Ryan. I now need you to do a bit of overtime for me. Find out every bit of information you can about him. Who he is, where he came from and what makes him tick. Tomorrow morning, I'm going to go and pay Mayor Lucas Fry a visit.'

27

DECEMBER 20TH

DS Patrick Howard was in a complete quandary. He was staring at a list of concert ticket purchases and the name that should have been against seat number six was not. There had been a major breach of crime site rules when the DCI had snatched that ticket off the forensics officer, and now he had a real problem. He wasn't in charge of this investigation. She was. If he tried to go above her head with this, what proof did he have?

There was the forensics officer's eye witness statement, but the DCI could just argue that it had been her ticket and he was mistaken in seeing seat six written on it. Was she manipulating the investigation in other ways? She certainly didn't like Dr Lane. Was that because she was worried he might see through her and work out what was going on? Maybe he already had. Harrison Lane was his only option. His only potential ally.

DS Howard texted him and said he would meet him at his hotel for breakfast; that there was something he needed to talk over. Harrison might assume it was the incident last night. Patrick knew he'd been about to punch Dougie, and Dougie was not the type to have let that go. He'd have had him up for brutality and excessive violence in an arrest. Harrison would have been hauled off the case and possibly off the NCA for good. He could have argued self-defence. Both Patrick and the uniformed officer that arrived with him had seen Dougie swing the punch first. Either way, he was glad the DCI hadn't been there.

When Patrick got to the hotel, he found Harrison had already arrived in the restaurant and claimed a table for them both. He'd just downed a glass of orange juice and was studying the menu.

'Going for the full English?' Patrick asked him as he slipped into the seat opposite.

'I am. Minus the black pudding and with scrambled eggs.' Harrison smiled.

'I think I'll join you. Need the fuel in weather like this.'

The pair of them looked out the window at the wintry scene. It had taken Patrick twice as long to get to the hotel, and that was on the main roads, which had been gritted. He'd passed a couple of cars along the way which had fallen foul of the black ice, but thankfully nothing serious.

A waitress hurried over to take their orders, and Patrick went to the tea and coffee machines to get himself a caffeine fix. Harrison joined him, taking a chamomile tea bag from the box of herbal teas. Patrick had sniffed one of them once, but that was about as close as he was ever planning to get to a herbal tea.

'You not drink coffee at all?' he asked Dr Lane.

Harrison shook his head.

Patrick didn't know what to make of the guy. Last night he'd been a mean fighting machine, and this morning he was sipping on herbal tea. What would Harrison make of what he was about to say? It was a risk for him. If he'd misjudged things, then it could have big repercussions for his career, but he couldn't just ignore it. Harrison had been there. Witnessed it. He was the only one he could talk to.

'What can I do for you?' Harrison asked him as they sat back down again.

The guy must have read his mind and was probably wondering why he'd invited himself to breakfast in the first place.

'I think...' he started, unsure of how to broach the topic. 'I need your advice on something.'

Harrison was studying his face. It unnerved him slightly, but at least he had his full attention.

'I don't know if you remember at the scrap yard? One of the forensics officers found something and showed it to the DCI and she took it. Said it was hers and must have blown out of her car.'

Harrison nodded slowly, still studying him.

'Well, obviously, that's against protocol, as I'm sure you know. But I also did a bit of digging and the ticket wasn't hers.'

'It was Lucas Fry's.' Harrison stated matter-of-factly.

The shock registered on Patrick's face.

'Yes. How did you know?'

'I did some digging, too. I'm glad that you've spoken to me about this because I know you're in a difficult position.'

Patrick slumped back in the chair in relief.

'Yeah. I mean, it could have blown out of her car. Maybe she gave him a lift home or something and he'd dropped it in her car and then...' Patrick stopped talking when he saw the look on Harrison's face.

'I've already decided to go round his house to have a chat. Straight after breakfast. There are a few things in his history which my assistant has flagged up. What I don't know is the DCI's involvement. She seems to want George Reid to take the blame and yesterday she effectively warned me off challenging her in any way. I knew you probably weren't her number one fan, but I wasn't sure exactly where you stood.'

Patrick hung his head and then looked out the window as though he'd find the words to answer him out there in the snow.

'She's not easy to work with,' he started, trying not to appear as though he was totally disloyal, but at the same time needing to appease his sense of duty. 'I've applied for transfers a couple of times, but she blocks them. I sometimes have concerns about what her agenda is.' He looked back at Harrison, who nodded.

'I think you're right to have those concerns. You're in a far more difficult position than me. My visit to Mr Fry may well stir up a hornets' nest and so it's probably better that you don't join me.'

Patrick shook his head. 'No. I'm not going to be afraid of her. I can stand up for myself. I want to come. This is our investigation and my territory. If you find anything of interest, it's best that you have a police officer with you.'

'OK,' Harrison replied.

Patrick was grateful that he didn't push the issue further. More important at that moment were the large plates of breakfast that had just arrived. They were going to need it. It was going to be another long day with no doubt yet more revelations.

28

DECEMBER 20TH

Lucas Fry lived on a large arable farm, in between two villages. Harrison left his hire car at the hotel and DS Howard drove them as conditions were difficult, and he was far more familiar with the roads.

'The land from here, on both sides of the road, is all Fry's,' he announced to Harrison as they got closer. 'He's a local lad, done good. Started with a run-down farm and has built up quite an empire. Has a scheme to employ some people with special needs in the farm shop and tries to get youngsters interested in farming. He also donates all the reject stock to local food banks. You know, anything that isn't quite the right shape and your middle-class shopper would turn their nose up to. He's a real social entrepreneur.'

Harrison looked out over vast fields covered in perfect, virgin snow. He wondered if a vicious killer could be the same person as the man who loved the land and helping his community.

It wasn't long before they came to a sign informing them that the farm shop entrance was just a hundred yards away on the right. As they rounded a bend, an entire complex of buildings rose up out of the white landscape. DS Howard indicated to turn in, although there were no other cars on the road. Most people had opted to stay indoors and work from home where possible. The English were not well-adapted to snowy conditions.

When they'd driven past the Home Fields Farm Shop and a series of outbuildings where workers could be seen preparing freshly harvested sprouts and other vegetables, they came to a small car parking area with a decent sized farmhouse in front of them.

'Big house for one man,' Harrison said.

'Yeah. I think his nephew lives somewhere on site or close by. He's been grooming him as his successor and I believe he runs the business mostly now, but Lucas still lives in the house.'

They scrunched through the crisp snow to the front door, following in the already trodden footprints of several before them. The second that Patrick knocked, a flurry of barking could be heard inside, which quickly grew closer before arriving behind the front door, closely followed by footsteps.

Lucas Fry edged open the door, holding on to the collar of a very exuberant chocolate Labrador.

'Mr Fry, DS Patrick Howard and Dr Harrison Lane, we wondered if we might have a word?'

'Yes, yes, we've met. But I haven't been introduced to Dr Lane before.' Lucas smiled at both men. 'Are you OK with dogs?'

'Yes, I'm fine,' Harrison replied.

'Errm, sometimes,' Patrick said, eyeing the brown lab. His voice sounded unconvincing.

'OK, let me just put Spud into the kitchen and we can go into the living room. Come on in.'

His manner was friendly and welcoming. He was clearly relaxed in his own home and had on brown corduroys and a taupe cable knit jumper – a change from the smart suit that Harrison had seen him in before.

Lucas Fry persuaded the reluctant Spud in through a door at the end of the entrance hall while Harrison and Patrick came inside and shut the cold out.

'This way, gentlemen,' Fry cheerfully waved them forward. 'Don't worry about your shoes. This is a farmhouse. Do you want a tea or coffee?'

'I wouldn't mind a tea, thank you,' the DS replied.

'Biscuits?' Lucas raised an eyebrow. 'They're made in the farm shop kitchen. Fresh shortbread.'

'Ah, sounds great, but no thanks. Just had a full English breakfast and not sure I'll be able to fit anything else in for at least a week.'

Lucas laughed. He wasn't coming across as a man who had something to hide.

'Dr Lane?'

'No, thank you. A glass of water is fine.'

'OK, find yourselves a seat and I'll go get our drinks.'

As they walked in, Harrison looked around the room. There was a painting of the farmhouse with what looked to be Lucas and a woman on the doorstep. He walked up to it, looking at the painted faces of Lucas and Ophelia Fry. Underneath the painting, on top of the sideboard, was a glass presentation case with small coins inside. Harrison peered at them. Roman.

On the far side of the room was a series of photographs featuring Ophelia at a location that looked out across the sea.

'Is that somewhere local?' Harrison asked DS Howard.

'It looks like Ness Point at Lowestoft. Most easterly point

of the UK. Lots of people go there for the view, especially at sunrise.'

There wasn't a TV in the room, but there was a CD player. Harrison looked at the rack of CDs. Mostly classical. It had been a while since he'd been somewhere where someone still listened to CDs and didn't have some kind of streaming device for their music.

The rest of the room was a comfortable, well-presented sitting room. The kind where you entertained, not curled up on the sofa to watch TV. A large ornate vase was sat atop a pedestal on the far side of the room, and Harrison wondered if the dog was ever allowed in here. An over-excited Labrador could easily bring that down. This was the public-facing side of Lucas Fry. The community ambassador. The mayor.

Lucas didn't take long to return to them with two mugs of milky tea and a glass of water.

'So, tell me what this is about. I'm guessing it has something to do with the church murders and fires? Terrible business,' he said, putting DS Howard's tea down on the table next to him and walking up to Harrison to hand him his water. 'I've offered whatever council resources we have to DCI Turner.'

'You and your wife?' Harrison asked, nodding at the painting of the house.

'Yes. Ops and I had that painted nearly twenty years ago now.'

'How long have you been here?' Harrison continued in a friendly tone. He and the DS had agreed that he'd lead the questioning, partly because if there was any flack after, then it would hopefully be aimed more at Harrison than him, but also because there were some specific details that Harrison wanted to check in relation to the profile he'd developed for their killer.

'I bought this farm thirty-two years ago. It wasn't much more than the house, which was in dire need of some TLC, and a couple of outbuildings plus two fields. Ops and I had to live in the kitchen and one bedroom for about four years while we saved the money to do it up. The priority was putting anything we earned into the business. Over the years, neighbouring farmers have retired and I've been able to buy up their land.'

'Your wife's name is Ops?' Harrison asked. He knew more than he was letting on, but wanted to hear Lucas Fry's explanation.

'Ophelia. I call her Ops.' He looked away from Harrison for a few moments. 'My wife passed away eighteen months ago.'

'I'm sorry for your loss. You must still miss her terribly.'

'Yes. Yes, I do. She was my partner in love, life, and business. We did everything together. I couldn't have done this without her. She loved this farm and the land, as do I.'

'Do your children help out with the farm?' Harrison asked.

'We were never blessed with children, Dr Lane,' Lucas replied.

Harrison didn't miss the twitching of his jaw or the slight inflection of his eyes.

'My nephew is my heir. He has been working with me for several years now. Basically runs the place, which is why I was able to start doing more for the community and ran for mayor.'

'Heir? You're still a young man!' Harrison replied. 'Surely you're not thinking of retiring yet?'

For the first time, he saw a slight slip of confidence and there was a hesitation before Lucas replied.

'No of course not, but when you've lost the love of your

life, it brings mortality so much closer. I just want to ensure that this can all continue with or without me. We employ around a hundred people here, more in our peak months. They rely on us. This farm and the land have meant everything to us. It's a part of me, a part of us. It's absolutely critical that I ensure its future. I know that's hard to understand if you're not a farmer. But to have my nephew, who is so dedicated to continuing that legacy, gives me a great feeling of security.'

Harrison nodded. 'I see you've found some archaeological treasures?'

'Yes. Roman coins. Found those myself when I was doing most of the graft in the fields in the early days.'

'Is that Saturn depicted on them?' Harrison asked.

'Yes, very well spotted, Dr Lane. For the Romans, Saturn was a King and then a god closely linked to agriculture, so I found it quite poetic that I'd discovered them in my fields. He had his own celebration, you know. A great time of feasting when the masters were supposed to serve the slaves.'

'It was around this time of year, wasn't it?' Harrison prompted him.

'Yes. It was.' Lucas eyed him curiously. 'Anyway, gentlemen, what did you come here for? Surely not to discuss my coin collection?'

Harrison smiled and followed Lucas to the sofas, sitting himself down at the opposite end to DS Howard, who threw him a look. He'd clearly heard their conversation.

Lucas put his tea down first and then sat down slightly awkwardly.

'Bad back,' he said to the two men, watching.

'As mayor, we wondered if you might have any idea what motive someone could have to commit these crimes. If you've heard anything through your community work.'

Lucas rubbed his left temple, wincing slightly as though he had a headache.

'I'm afraid I don't. DCI Turner has already asked me.'

'Are you a regular churchgoer, Mr Fry?'

Harrison could see him weighing up his answer.

'I wouldn't say we were regular. I go to the main services – you know, Thanksgiving and Christmas, Easter etc. – but as mayor I need to embrace all religions. I also attend Diwali celebrations, for example.'

'Ah yes, you were at the carol service weren't you, the evening that the fire was started at St Mary's?'

'I was.'

'Were you also helping with the removal of boxes from the two fire-hit churches?'

'I was one of several who brought boxes over. Reverend Davenport asked me to. He knew I was coming to the service and so asked if I could bring some boxes on my way.'

'Who else was there helping? Can you remember?'

'Well, yes, there was Reverend Davenport, George, the chap who looks after the graveyards, Trudy somebody, who is one of the vergers from St Mary's, and Reverend Galloway. I think others had helped too, but I only saw them when I was there.'

'And you were in the congregation when the explosion happened?'

'Yes. In the front row with the headmaster. I have to say everyone worked very well together, making sure the children were all evacuated safely.'

'Yes, it could have been catastrophic with all those children there.'

Lucas looked slightly uncomfortable at that question and rubbed at his head again. 'Well, there wasn't any immediate danger. The fire was in the back. There was a door between us and the explosion was only small. Science teachers do similar experiments in labs up and down the country.'

'Similar experiments to what, Mr Fry?' Harrison looked dead pan at the mayor and waited for him to realise that he'd just said something he shouldn't actually know.

The penny dropped.

'You know, chemical explosions for dramatic effect. Someone told me that's what it was.'

'Who told you that?' DS Howard asked now, adding to Lucas's discomfort.

'I think it was one of the fire officers. Look, I'm not going to name names. I don't want to get anyone into trouble.'

'I see.' Harrison smiled at him, noting the rapid eye blinks which indicated he was struggling to keep his story going. 'So you went outside with everyone?'

He nodded eagerly, relieved to get away from the topic but still looking like a cornered mouse that had managed to escape the claws of the cat once, but knew danger was still very much present.

'Did you notice at what time Reverend Davenport disappeared?'

'I didn't I'm afraid.' Lucas rubbed at his temple again and then his eyes.

'Are you alright, Mr Fry?' Harrison asked.

'Yes, I'm fine. It's been quite a traumatic week all in all. I've just got a bit of a headache.'

'So you didn't notice when Reverend Davenport left. So where were you while the fire was being attended to? Were you there throughout?'

'I was there reassuring people. Everyone wants to talk when things like this are going on. It's my job to serve our community.'

'We've looked on the attending police officers' body cam

footage and we can't see you. Can you tell me where you were standing?'

'Why?'

'It just helps us place everyone at the scene so we can try to work out who might have seen Reverend Davenport leave.'

'Well, I moved around. I can't just say I was in one position, but DCI Turner might remember. When she arrived, she saw me.'

'DCI Turner saw you there?'

'Yes, ask her.' Lucas stuck out his chin in defiance.

'Could I ask you where you were the night of the fire at St Luke's?'

The expression on Lucas Fry's face changed, his features becoming slightly harder and his eyes fixed onto Harrison.

'I was here. On my own with Spud.'

'Can anyone verify that for you?'

'No. Why would they need to? What is this with all these questions? It's as though you think I might be involved.'

'We are just being thorough, checking everyone who was at those locations. But that's all for now. Thank you for your time and if you do think of anything that might help the inquiry, then please let us know.'

Lucas Fry got up awkwardly from the chair and went to show them out.

'Did you enjoy the concert at the town hall last week?' Harrison asked him before leaving.

'The concert?' There was a pause. 'Do you mean the classical music recital? Yes, I did thank you. I enjoy singing and classical music. It's quite therapeutic. But why do you ask and how did you know I went?'

Harrison didn't answer immediately. He waited until the front door was fully open and they were about to leave.

'It's our job to know, Mr Fry.'

With that the two men walked out, leaving Lucas Fry staring after them.

'Well, that's sure to put the cat among the pigeons!' DS Howard whispered to Harrison on the way down the path. 'You weren't entirely as subtle as I thought you'd be. He's going to be straight on the phone to the DCI.'

'I suspect so. But as you know, when people are scared, they can make mistakes.'

'So, how did he know about the explosion? Do you reckon the DCI told him or one of the fire officers as he said?'

'Personally, I reckon it's because he did it.'

DS Howard thought for a few moments. 'Have to say, it's too coincidental that he knows all about that Roman god who you said used to be celebrated at Christmas time.'

'Not only that, but he calls his wife Ops. Ops was the name of Saturn's wife. Did you notice that he didn't have a scrap of anything related to Christmas in his house? No cards up, no decorations. Nothing.'

'He might not feel like celebrating, having lost his wife.'

'True, but this is his second Christmas without her. You'd have thought he might have at least put on some kind of public display even if he doesn't feel like celebrating himself. Plus, as mayor, he'd be getting plenty of cards.'

'Well, he makes a lousy cup of tea. The milk was off.' Patrick sulked as he got into the car.

'Really? That's interesting,' Harrison said to him. 'His left side seems a little weaker, and he also seems to be suffering from headaches. He drank his tea quite happily, which suggests that he didn't taste the milk was off.'

'Yeah, he did sit down awkwardly. What could it all mean?'

'Perhaps he has a medical issue. It could also explain his preoccupation with finding an heir.'

'Maybe, but what does that have to do with our case?'

'People who know they are dying sometimes want to settle old scores. A life sentence for him would hardly be a problem if he was caught.'

'So we seriously need to consider that he could be our killer? The mayor? He genuinely seems like a really good bloke.'

'Yes. I think we definitely need to consider him.'

'But why? What would he have against the church and the vicars? He knows them, talks to them. He's worked really hard to be a part of this community and gives so much to it.'

'Yes, and doesn't the evidence point to someone who the vicars knew. There was no struggle, they went willingly with their killer. His wife Ophelia's death could have unhinged him slightly. Perhaps it was something to do with her?'

'I don't know what to think. I just can't believe that man in there could do what was done to Reverend Soulsby and Davenport.'

'Monsters can lurk inside of all of us, DS Howard. A career in the police force should have proven that to you.'

'I know. It's just usually I can spot the signs. You know, you get a feel for someone's personality and behaviour.'

'With Lucas Fry, assuming it is him, it will be extremely personal and extremely focused. It will be a tiny part of him which is committing these crimes and it will be quarantined away from the majority of his personality, which is Lucas Fry the mayor and champion of the community. He will have a justification for it, which fits with his own moral code.

'Most criminals, although not all, have something inside of them which wants to do good. They understand right and wrong and what is and isn't moral. It's just they justify their actions against that moral code. Whether it's a thief who thinks that it's social justice that somebody shouldn't have something that they haven't, or a murderer who believes the person they are killing has wronged them in some way. Lucas Fry may be mostly good, but a part of him has turned murderous and something will have triggered that – and, in his own mind, it is totally justified.'

'Have to say he was quite defensive when you suggested that the little explosion and fire at St Luke's could have hurt the children.'

'Yup. I'd expect most people to be railing against what happened, angry that whoever did it had potentially put young lives at risk, but he played it down. Said there hadn't been any real risk to the kids. That's another indicator for me.'

Patrick looked at him, deep in thought. 'But we've no solid evidence against him.'

'No. And that's the problem. It's as weak as the DCI's case against George; nothing but circumstantial evidence. He fits the profile, though. Perfectly. I've just got to figure out the motive, and fast. It's the eve of the solstice tonight. If we don't stop him soon, then it might be too late.'

29

DECEMBER 20TH

DS Howard dropped Harrison back at his hotel so that he could pick up his car to check in on George Reid. It was partly a welfare call, to see if he was alright after last night's events, partly an information-gathering exercise.

The snow had thankfully decided to give it a rest, and while the roads were still fairly treacherous, the gritters had been out and progress was much easier. When Harrison arrived, he could still see the signs of last night's unwelcome visitors. The Christmas wreath, which had been on George's door, was just about visible as small bits of green and red poking through the white path and garden. Where the men had stamped around, or the winter sun had managed to melt the snow a little, the snow cover was thinner and harder and the remains of the wreath showed. A bright red and green reminder of their bigotry.

Harrison knocked on the door.

'George, Mr Reid? It's Dr Harrison Lane. We met at All Saints and I was here last night with the police.'

He saw the curtain move very slightly in the downstairs window and Harrison stepped back from the door to ensure George could get a good look at him. The man would be very wary. He didn't want to make him even more anxious.

Half a minute later, the front door semi-opened and George peered out at him.

'Would you mind if I came in for a few minutes?'

George looked behind him as if to check on the place and then opened the door to let him in.

Harrison found himself in a small sitting room area that had probably been decorated at some point in the eighties and not touched since. There was a small open fire which was lit, plus two old armchairs and a table with a further two chairs. One of the chairs was draped with an all-weather jacket; the one Harrison had seen him in two days ago. The carpet had probably not seen a hoover in some time. George had nobody to tell him to take his muddy boots off when he got home.

'You OK?' Harrison asked him.

George gave a small nod and stared at the orange fire in front of them.

'I know you have nothing to do with this, so please don't think I'm here to catch you out about anything. I wanted to be sure you were OK after last night and to see if you could help me.'

George looked up at him.

'Thank you for stopping them,' he said.

Harrison felt a pang of pure sympathy for the man. He could feel the pain leaching out of him. His world had collapsed in just a few days. Two of his beloved churches destroyed, three people he worked with murdered, and the officer leading the investigation was trying to point the finger at him.

'Don't think that they represent what the community is thinking. They were just a tiny minority and they won't bother you again. We are going to find the real killer and your name will be cleared.'

George wrapped his arms around his torso defensively. 'DCI Turner doesn't agree with you. She thinks it was me.'

'Mmh, I think there may be reasons behind that. It's why I need your help.'

George sat himself upright in his chair, ready. 'OK...'

'Do you go to many of the services?'

He nodded. 'Every week. I take it in turns. I like to be a part of each church.'

'Have you seen the mayor and his wife at any services?'

George frowned, thinking.

'The mayor only goes to the big ones. I think it's because he thinks he should be seen. He never prays, you know. Doesn't even sing. I sat near to him once and he just opens and closes his mouth. He always smiles at the vicar and talks to everyone, but he doesn't take part.'

'What about his wife?'

George shook his head. 'I never saw her. Not once. Not even at Christmas. Her parents used to come when they were alive. I think she'd been in the choir once when she was younger.'

'What about her funeral?'

George shook his head again and shrugged his shoulders.

'It wasn't at any of our churches. I think it was a quiet one on account of the circumstances.'

'Circumstances?'

'Yeah. I heard that she'd taken her own life. Had issues for years, apparently.'

'You never met her?'

'No. She didn't leave the farm much.'

Harrison thought for a moment while George stared into the flames of his fire.

'You helped bring the boxes over from the burnt churches to St Mary's. Did you see Lucas Fry then?'

'Yes. He brought a few over from St Luke's. He'd offered, said it was on his way in.'

'He offered, are you sure? Reverend Davenport didn't ask him?'

'No. It was definitely his suggestion. We'd pretty much got it sorted between us but Reverend Davenport didn't want to upset him, so he'd agreed. I was with the vicar when the mayor called him.'

'You've been very helpful, George. Thank you.'

'I have?' George's face lit up with a smile for the first time.

'One more question. How would somebody have got hold of the keys to get into All Saints? Where are spare copies kept?'

'Usually it's just the vicars, the vergers, and me. But with All Saints, because there's no vicar been appointed yet, there was a spare set which had been in the vestry. I told Reverend Galloway that on the Monday I'd gone in and couldn't see the spare keys.'

'Why Reverend Galloway?'

'He'd conducted the service there the day before.'

'What did he say?'

'He said that somebody must have borrowed them.'

'He didn't seem concerned?'

George shook his head.

'Did you tell this to the police?'

'Yes.'

'Was the mayor at the All Saints service the day before?'

George paused a moment to think.

'Yes. Yes, he was. He sat next to Mrs Riveley, who does the

church flowers. She was pleased about that. I remember her talking about it afterwards.'

Their chat was interrupted by a knock at the door. George looked at Harrison, fright flashing in his eyes. Harrison smiled kindly to reassure him and let him know he was there if needed. George took a deep breath and got up from his chair and crossed to the door.

Harrison also got up. If there was going to be any trouble, he'd need to be ready for it.

'George. We were terribly sorry to hear about your troubles last night. We've come to see that you're OK and brought you a casserole and a Victoria sponge. We know you like a slice of cake. Mr Watson is going to pop around later with a new wreath for you from the garden centre.'

At the front door were two ladies, who Harrison estimated to be in their sixties, maybe even early seventies, with kind, warm faces.

'Mrs Peterson, Mrs Edwards. That's so...' George's voice faltered. Their kind gesture was the final straw in an emotional roller coaster few days.

'George, I'll say goodbye,' Harrison said to him. 'Why don't you invite the ladies in and I'll get out of your way?'

George just nodded and shuffled aside from the doorway. The two women appraised Harrison as he appeared in the bright, snowy light. He smiled politely and scrunched away down the path, happy that George's community was now uniting to support him. Behind him, he could hear the two women chatting away and rallying George along. He'd be fine. Now, Harrison needed to deal with the source of his problems. That would take a little more work than a slice of Victoria sponge.

30

DECEMBER 20TH

Ryan had spent a restless night with barely any sleep. He jolted awake at the slightest sound. Disturbed by nightmares that came from his past but which threatened his future. Addie had been knocking on the door again yesterday evening, and this time he'd had company. There was no longer any pretence at having a chat and being friends. Their language had been direct and threatening. They wanted him to do a job for them and they wanted it done soon. He had twenty-four hours to open his door and speak to them before they broke it down.

Ryan had been mulling over his options. There was only one way into and out of this building, apart from the fire escape at the back, and that was a narrow metal staircase, which clanged with each footstep – and wasn't designed for removing household contents. The whole block of flats could hear when somebody was going up or down it.

The gang wasn't totally stupid. They'd be watching his flat.

He had thousands of pounds' worth of computer equipment in here; there was no way he was abandoning it. He looked around, estimating how long it would take him to pack up and get out. Two hours tops. He still had all the boxes from the move here. But there was no way he'd be able to carry everything himself and even if he tried, they'd stop him.

Who was he kidding, anyway? His agoraphobia would ensure he didn't just up and leave, and they knew it.

He almost missed the call from Harrison. It had been his boss's third attempt. With his mobile on silent, Ryan just hadn't seen it.

'Ryan. What's up? You OK?'

'No. Fine. Yeah, I'm fine.' Even to somebody who didn't know Ryan well, let alone his friend and the man who was adept at understanding human nature, it was clear he was anything but fine.

'What's going on, Ryan? You need to tell me.' Harrison's voice took on a new tone. This time he wasn't friendly. He was authoritative.

Ryan knew he couldn't hide the truth from him any longer. Not only was it impacting his work, but in another twenty-four hours, he might not even be here to explain it.

'They've found me.'

There was a silence on the phone.

'Addie's girlfriend lives on the ground floor. He saw me.'

'And he knows it's you for sure?'

'Yeah, he's been knocking on my door every day. They want me to do a job for them. If I don't do as they say, then they're coming in to make me. I don't know what to do.'

'You pack. I'll sort it.'

'How? They're going to be watching my flat.'

'I'll sort it, Ryan. I promise. Just pack and be ready. I'll call you in a bit.'

'I'm sorry.'

'This is not your fault. We checked out the other residents as best we could. We knew this could happen sometime.'

'But I'm supposed to be helping you with this case.'

'You've helped already. Let's get you sorted out and then you can carry on. You're no good to me or yourself if you're back with them, or, worse still, dead.'

'You've got so much to deal with already.'

'I can't come. Not yet, but I'll send people I trust. You'll be safe. Pack up and I'll call soon with instructions.'

The phone went dead and Ryan sat there for a few moments, wishing his boss and friend was here with him, not miles away in Suffolk. His anxiety levels had set his heart racing and when he finally stood up, his head felt light. He had to do as Harrison had told him. He wouldn't let him down.

Ryan walked into his bedroom where the cardboard boxes he had were stored and began his evacuation.

31

DECEMBER 20TH

Hearing Ryan so frightened had hit Harrison in the guts. He'd sat in his car outside George's house and tried to calm his emotions so that he could think clearly. It had been a long time since he'd heard Ryan sound so lost and afraid, and the worst part was that he wasn't there to be able to help him. He'd run through some ideas in his mind, some of which involved him heading straight back to London. That was a final resort. He didn't want to turn his back on the victims, their families, and George. He had no faith in the DCI and while DS Howard was a good officer, he couldn't fight her alone. She'd play dirty.

He remembered Addie from their first encounter. In fact, Addie still carried around the healed fractures in his jawbone and right arm, courtesy of Harrison. It had been that or a knife in his own chest. For the last few years, he and Ryan had been careful to ensure he was never anywhere that they could find him. It wasn't as if Ryan went out much. His condition meant he spent most of his time either in his flat or at the office.

They'd checked out the tenants in his new flat thoroughly before Ryan had moved. He'd needed somewhere that was close to their new offices; he could only manage a short walk outside, and it had to be familiar. They'd had no way of knowing that Addie's girlfriend was in the flats. They needed to be more careful going forward.

Harrison's immediate concern was to get Ryan out of there and to somewhere safe. Somewhere that the gang wouldn't know to look for him. The where was easy. It was the how that was slightly harder. Ryan was right. They'd be watching the flat.

Getting the police involved wasn't an option. If Addie's gang knew that Ryan was working with the police, then not only would he become useless to them, but he'd become a liability. They might also figure out that he was somehow involved in the series of arrests that had taken place across their network several years ago when he'd disappeared.

Just moving out wasn't going to be an option, either. The second he set foot outside, they'd pounce. He'd be taken and anyone helping him would end up in the hospital. That was, unless you were somebody who knew how to fight and defend yourself against low-lifes like Addie and his gang. Harrison knew just the guy. Within fifteen minutes, it was sorted. He called Ryan back and told him to be ready to leave at 4 p.m. Someone called Calvin would knock on his door and he should have an overnight bag ready, too. He was to do everything that Calvin told him to do.

Worrying about Ryan was a distraction that he could do without, but Harrison was at least reassured that Calvin would deal with it. He also called their friend, DS Jack Salter, to give him the heads up, but warned him not to get involved. Addie and his mates could spot a police officer a mile off. It wouldn't be good for him or Ryan. Instead, he asked Jack for a favour.

The quicker he could get this case wrapped up, the quicker he could get back to London. Harrison tried to put it out of his mind and focus on Suffolk. As he drove back to the incident room, he ran through what he knew. He was convinced that the killer wanted to highlight that the church hid the truth. Why else go to all the trouble of leaving the pottery statues in order to link to Saturnalia and the usurping of Christmas?

There had to be a case where the killer had tried to expose something and the church had denied it, or hidden it. There were countless cases of child abuse within various churches over the years, most covered over and never dealt with until more recent times. Could it be one of these? Could Lucas Fry have been a victim of abuse?

He'd just arrived back at the incident room car park when DI Seb Bartholomew at the NCA rang.

'Harrison, you're obviously doing a good job down there. DCI Turner has put in a formal complaint and requested that you be taken off the case.'

'Complaint about what?'

'Said you were harassing witnesses.'

Harrison smiled. 'Interesting. It didn't take her long. I don't know what her involvement is, but I thought that I was on to something and if she has reacted this quickly, then that just makes me think I'm definitely right.'

'What? You mean that she's involved in all this somehow?'

'I'm not saying she's committing the crimes, but she might be protecting someone.'

'Well, I've filed her request for now, but tread carefully. She is the officer in charge and you're on her patch. You don't want to be eating one of their custody suite meals for Christmas lunch.'

When Harrison arrived in the incident room, the team was in a briefing. A briefing that he hadn't been informed about. George's face was plastered up on the board and the DCI had been listing all the evidence against him. She looked across to Harrison as he walked in, and glared.

He searched for DS Howard and walked over to where he was leaning against the side wall.

The DS raised his eyebrows in greeting. 'She's on the warpath,' he whispered. 'Lucas must have called her straight after we left. I told her that I was just following the instructions she'd given us at the last briefing. To talk to everyone who had been moving the boxes across to St Mary's. I think she bought that but wasn't happy with your line of questioning.'

'She's tried to get me kicked off the case,' Harrison whispered back.

DS Howard looked at him, alarmed.

'It isn't happening,' Harrison reassured him.

The DCI looked over their way, frowning.

'Do we have your full attention, DS Howard?' she shouted across.

'Yes, ma'am,' he replied, straightening up from where he'd been leaning in to whisper to Harrison.

Harrison stayed staring straight at her, not breaking his gaze. Her eyes tried to bore into his, but he didn't let them in. She broke contact and continued with the briefing.

'We know from George's social services records that he was passed from one home to another after being beaten nearly to death by his father at a young age. This clearly ties into the way in which Reverend Soulsby was murdered. I'm sure Dr Lane, over there, would agree that people sometimes commit crimes based on deep-rooted childhood traumas.'

Harrison said nothing. She continued anyway. 'I want a detailed breakdown of George Reid's movements over the past five days. I don't want a minute of that man's life unaccounted for. Get to it.'

HARRISON WASN'T ABOUT to get into a confrontation with DCI Turner. He was on edge enough as it was with worrying about Ryan. And he had the case to concentrate on.

His conversation with George had given him an idea. Until he had something firm, he was going to do it alone. No point risking DS Howard's career. He logged into the computer and looked up a coroner's report. Then, as the incident room buzzed around him and DS Howard was in a small meeting with some other officers, he slipped out to have another conversation with the forensic pathologist, Dr Oliver Charles.

THE MORTUARY TECHNICIAN, Amelia Smith, opened the door for Harrison and showed him through to the DOC's office. She looked a little different today than their last encounter; she was wearing make-up and had changed her hair. Harrison wondered if maybe she was going out on a date later.

The DOC was neatly folded into his chair behind his desk, working on the latest report.

'Dr Lane,' he greeted him, 'what can I do for you today? I've just about finished the full report on Reverend Davenport. We're waiting on a few toxicology results, but they'll be a little while yet.'

'It's not Reverend Davenport I'm here about.' Harrison got straight to the point. 'I wanted to ask you about another autopsy you undertook about eighteen months ago.'

DOC leaned forward on his desk and furrowed his brow, listening.

'Ophelia Fry. I understand that she might have committed suicide.'

'Ah yes, the unfortunate Mrs Fry. Such a shame. Her husband was devastated. He found her. Wait a moment and I'll get up the full report to refresh my memory. How does this connect to our recent visitors?'

'I can't say at present. It is a line of inquiry I'm following.'

'OK, fair enough. Here we go. She had been cutting herself for years. Her poor arms were scarred, and her legs too. Most of the scarring was quite old. It looked like she'd had bouts of depression and, from the evidence given at the inquest, I understand that she had very low self-esteem and struggled to socialise. She died after cutting her wrists and bleeding out in the bath. It was straightforward. I didn't see any evidence of foul play, and nothing was raised by the police.'

'Nothing unusual at all?'

'Well, yes. But not directly related to her death. We ran a digital CT scan on her as there was no need for an invasive autopsy and that shows us all her internal organs. At some point, and this will be a long time ago due to the healing and scarring, Mrs Fry had a hysterectomy. But it wasn't that which was unusual, it was the evidence of other internal damage in that area.'

Harrison looked quizzical.

'I've seen similar cases before when a woman has either

undertaken an abortion herself, or gone to some back-street quack to get it done. Whoever did this to her made a real mess of it.'

'Any idea when this might have taken place?'

'Difficult for me to say, but you're talking many years. It was old and healed scarring. I'd say she was young, potentially not yet into full adulthood by the way her body changed around the healed areas. Perhaps it could explain some of her depression, as the poor woman certainly couldn't ever have children again. No doubt would have played havoc with the hormones, too.'

'Did her medical records show this in her history?'

DOC shook his head. 'No. No mention of it, which again leads me to suspect it was a fair time ago, or possibly out of this area. A professional must have patched her up, so I'd have thought at some point she ended up in a hospital.'

'Thank you, Doctor Charles. That's been very helpful.' Harrison got up to leave. 'Actually, I know this isn't quite your bag but I wonder if you could give me some advice about some symptoms I've noticed in an individual.'

'I'll do what I can to help Dr Lane, but it will be guess-work without a proper diagnosis and as you know I deal more with the dead than the living.'

Fifteen minutes later, Harrison exited the morgue and immediately dialled DS Howard's number.

'We need to talk.'

32

DECEMBER 20TH

Ryan was ready to undo the last of his make-shift barricade, on the dot at 4 p.m. Behind him, his life had been thrown into the boxes it had only recently been taken out of. He wasn't somebody who liked to leave his home, but he'd never felt more ready to get out of this place.

His ears strained to hear any sounds from downstairs. Addie could strike at any moment. When the intercom door buzzer sounded, right by his head, it made him jump about two feet off the floor.

'It's Calvin. Harrison sent me.'

Ryan pressed the entry button and started counting in his head as his anxiety levels rose to the ceiling. He ripped the last home-made lock off the door and as he heard the heavy footsteps reach his top floor, he opened it.

Ryan peered through the gap allowed by the security chain on his flat door, and saw a man dressed in green fatigues. He wasn't as big as Harrison, but one glance was enough to tell him that he was fit. His blond hair was cut

short around his ears and neck, which was thick and muscular. Ryan couldn't see his face properly because he wore a
surgical mask like the ones everyone had to wear for Covid. It
didn't look out of place, but it served to hide his identity.

'Ryan?' the man asked him.

'Yes,' he replied, undoing the chain on the door.

'Which flat does Addie stay in?'

'Two.'

'This him?' Calvin took out his phone and showed Ryan a
photograph. It was Addie, a shot taken of him walking down
the street, unaware that he was being photographed.

He nodded.

'OK. Let me see how much stuff you've got.'

Ryan opened the door fully to let Calvin come in. He took
seconds to appraise the boxes.

'You stay up here. We'll have someone with you at all
times. There's five of us. One will stay with the van, the rest of
us will take it in turns to bring this lot downstairs. We've all
got radios. You take this one, just in case, but it shouldn't be
necessary.'

Calvin thrust a small black walkie-talkie at Ryan. Then he
spoke into his own, which had been clipped to his belt.

'Ready to rock.'

It was all like some kind of a surreal dream for Ryan. He'd
been holed-up in the flat without seeing a single human
being for days, and now a succession of big muscular men
were walking in and picking up his belongings. Calvin was
true to his word. They never left him alone, making sure that
while the others were on the stairs or loading the van,
someone was in the flat.

It didn't take long before the expected trouble began.

'What you after, mate?' Ryan heard one of the men on the
stairs.

'I live here – I'm going to my flat.' It was Addie's voice.

'Yeah? Well, that's number two, ain't it? Which, if I ain't mistaken, is on the ground floor.'

Calvin had briefed them well. The man who was in the flat with Ryan moved to the doorway.

'You can't stop me from going upstairs.' Addie had totally misjudged the situation. He probably thought the guy was a normal removals man and would be intimidated.

'I think I can, actually.' The guy stood firm.

Ryan could hear more footsteps on the stairs.

'You don't want to pick a fight, Addie mate. It won't end too good for you.' It was Calvin's voice.

There was a pause, and then Addie swore. He said a few choice words about Calvin's mother and retreated back downstairs.

Calvin was in the flat within seconds.

'Right, we need to really move things now. He'll be calling in backup.'

They were around half-way through the boxes. Ryan realised he'd started to shake. Adrenaline and lack of decent food over the last few days were getting the better of him.

'They do drive-bys,' Ryan said to Calvin. 'They wouldn't think twice.'

'I know. We've fixed that. The road's blocked. The only way they can get to us is on foot.'

That thought made Ryan feel better for all of five seconds as the image of a car-load of gun-wielding drug gang members driving by and spraying them all with bullets disappeared from the list of possibilities. It didn't, however, take long for his imagination to find them all getting out of the car with their guns and running along the road.

The men worked fast and there were just a couple of boxes left when Calvin reappeared.

'You got your bag?' he asked Ryan.

He nodded nervously.

'OK. Let's go. The boys will get these last two. Does the door lock automatically, or do we need keys?'

'You just need to pull it closed.'

'Right. Come on, let's get you out of here.'

Ryan held on to the stair rail for dear life, his legs turned to jelly. His agoraphobia made this a tough enough journey without the threat of Addie and his gang. When they reached the first landing, there was a large box, like the wardrobe boxes that removals men used, only this one had been reinforced inside with metal, and had air holes.

'You going to be ok getting in there?' Calvin said to him, nodding at the box.

For a few seconds, Ryan panicked. 'Why?' he asked.

'We've got three vans outside,' Calvin whispered, mindful that someone further down the stairs might be listening. 'Boxes are going in each one. You're going in as a box. They won't know that we've got you, and it's going to be hard for them to follow all three vans.'

It was a simple ruse, but Ryan could see how easily it might work.

'You can breathe and see through the holes.'

'It's fine. I don't get claustrophobic. I actually like small spaces,' Ryan replied, stepping forward and getting into the box. It was a comfy fit. He turned round and watched as Calvin closed the door and sealed it.

'See you soon,' Calvin winked at him reassuringly.

The box had several holes in it, which he hadn't been able to see clearly from the outside because they'd been carefully concealed amid the writing on the outside. While the view was limited, he could see in all directions.

When he heard footsteps come up the stairs, he turned and saw one of Calvin's men arrive on the landing.

'Main cargo,' Calvin said to him and he saw a nod of acknowledgement. 'Here we go,' Calvin added, which he knew was meant for him. The box tipped back and was then hoisted up at both ends.

The two men walked slowly down the stairs, carrying their precious cargo. Through the holes, Ryan felt the chill air blast from the main doors as they got to the ground floor. He'd not been outside at all for days and it felt cold, even wrapped up in his metal box.

'Last two boxes upstairs,' Calvin said to someone, and he saw the flash of a person heading into the building.

Ryan couldn't see too clearly, but the road seemed to be filled with white vans. His box was gently placed on the road behind one of them. He waited for the movement as he was hoisted into the van, but it didn't come. Instead, he heard Calvin's radio. 'Incoming Poulson Street end. They're carrying.'

'Here we go,' Calvin said to the man with him. Ryan heard van doors slam. He strained to see through the tiny holes in his box. One looked straight at the front door to his building. The front and back holes allowed him to see up and down the road. Coming up the road from the Poulson Street end, he could just see a group of hooded thugs. He knew what 'carrying' meant. Whoever had been lookout at the top of the road knew they had guns.

He was terrified. Not only for his own life, but for Calvin and the rest of the men. He'd read the headlines of shootings and stabbings in London. The drugs gangs didn't care about who got hurt as long as they got what they wanted and kept control of their territories. They wanted Ryan, and as far as they were concerned, they thought he was probably still holed up in his flat.

The last two of Calvin's men had exited the building with the remaining boxes, which they put down beside his.

'We need to keep 'em busy if we can,' Calvin said to them. 'Remember the plan. Are the other boxes ready?'

'Sorted.'

'Right, Dave and Kieran, in you go. Lee, pass me one of our boxes.'

By now the gang was getting close and Ryan could see that at least two of them had their hands in their trouser waistlines, ready to pull out weapons. There was movement in the building doorway. Addie appeared. He motioned to the gang to come in.

Ryan heard shouting from inside.

'Come on, we need to get out of here quick. Move.' He couldn't understand who was shouting it and why.

What was going on?

They were outnumbered. Now, he could see seven, plus Addie. Eight of them.

Ryan's heart was beating so hard and fast he thought it would burst right out of his chest. His breathing was fast and shallow. He was struggling to get in enough air. What if he got trapped in the box? How was he going to get out? Images of being sealed in a container right in the middle of a gunfight flew around his brain and sent his blood pressure higher. The urge to panic and try to get out was hard to resist.

As the gang came up to them, Ryan saw Addie raise his arm in the doorway. Followed by several flashes as he fired his gun. Straight at Calvin.

Calvin was fast. He'd also seen the movement and had dived. As he did so, the box he was holding burst open and two taser gun wires came out from it, heading straight towards the front row of the gang. The other two removal men's boxes did the same. Four of the gang fell to the floor writhing as several of the taser darts found their marks.

Addie had disappeared back inside. Ryan guessed he was probably heading up the stairs to his flat, thinking he was still in there.

One of the other gang members lunged at the nearest removal man with a jagged steel knife. With lightning rapid movements, the man deflected the incoming blow and had the guy on the ground in the blink of an eye. The other two gang members ran into the building, waving their guns and shooting indiscriminately.

Calvin and his men detached the tasers and dragged the incapacitated hoodies into the building entrance after the rest of their gang. Their guns and knives went with them. Then the door was closed and a steel bar slotted through the two handles. It meant that nobody would be able to leave.

From Ryan's left, he saw more movement. The other two removals men coming from the opposite end of the road. In the distance, he heard multiple sirens.

Before he knew it, he was being hoisted into the back of the van. There were two more thumps as the other boxes were chucked in after him, and then the doors clanged shut. Within seconds, he heard doors slamming in the front and then the engine roared into life and they were moving. From here on in he could see and hear nothing, apart from the white interior roof of the van, the brown boxes stacked around him and the sound of the van's engine which quickly slowed to normal speed and made its way through the traffic of London. They were away, but where was he being taken?

33

DECEMBER 20TH

Harrison was on tenterhooks while he waited for DS Howard to meet him in the cafe by the incident room. Not because of the case or any concerns about the DCI finding out, but because he was waiting to hear if the operation to extract Ryan from his flat had been successful.

He had every faith in Calvin and his men, but sometimes even the best-laid plans could go awry.

The call came right on schedule.

'All targets in custody and your parcel has been delivered safely.' The phone went dead.

Harrison and Calvin knew not to talk about what had just been arranged on a mobile phone. That one sentence was all he'd needed.

DS Howard walked up just as Harrison relaxed back into the chair with relief.

'Alright?' the DS asked him.

'All good,' Harrison said, switching straight back into

business mode. 'I think I might have found the motive. We've just got to prove it.'

'Ah, that little chestnut. Proof. The bane of our lives.'

Harrison looked at Patrick's face, frowning.

'Sorry, I was joking. Just trying to lighten the mood. It's been a tough few days. My wife's at home with our daughter, who has just reached the age when she gets all the Christmas stuff. She's hyper and I'm not even around to share it or to help.'

For a moment, DS Howard had let slip his perfectly practiced professionalism and shared a little of his private life. The manicured appearance which protected his inner thoughts and tribulations remained intact, but his face and body language told the story. Harrison felt for him. Having a boss like DCI Turner must be a terrible strain. It was obvious she wouldn't respect family time.

'We'll get this sorted. I think we're close,' Harrison reassured him.

Patrick nodded and sighed.

'I need you to check the diocese records. Find out when Reverend Soulsby and Davenport came to the area and who else was around at the time.'

'That's easy. I can do that without the DCI being suspicious. What else?'

'Ask if there's been any complaints logged against any of them for abuse or assault, the usual.'

'I think that has already been done for our two victims, and there was nothing on record. I'll check for the others.'

'Don't forget to include Bishop Warriner in that.'

'OK. What are you going to do next?'

'I'm going to go pay some social calls.'

34

DECEMBER 20TH

Harrison returned to Lucas Fry's farm. The shop had half an hour before it was closing and so he figured it was likely to be quiet. He pretended to be browsing, looking for an opportunity to get chatting with the staff. His mind wasn't exactly on Christmas shopping, but there were some locally made gifts available. It was one range, in particular, which caught his eye. A series of hand-made terracotta garden ornaments. There were toads and hedgehogs, and various birds, cats and dogs, but it was the female figurines which particularly interested him. They were in the Roman or Italian style. There wasn't anything that looked exactly like the figurines they'd found at the crime scenes, but they were similar.

As he wandered round the shop, he was immediately attracted to the beautiful scent of the hyacinths, and partly to give himself an excuse to chat to the cashier, he chose a nice-looking lantern display with several of the bulbs about to burst into flower. He could give it to Jack's wife, Marie, when they went round for Christmas lunch.

The shop only had about three other people in it, despite it being peak festive shopping time, and that was almost certainly down to the weather.

'It's quiet in here,' Harrison said to the cashier as he gave her the planter, trying to strike up a conversational relationship.

She was a woman who looked as though she hadn't had an easy life. Although she was probably only in her early forties, she looked older. Her face was heavily lined and her hands were the same. The tip of a scar could just be seen poking through her hairline on her forehead.

'Yeah. Snow been keeping everyone indoors,' she replied. 'I don't mind. We been rushed off our feet these past weeks.'

'Do Lucas and Ophelia Fry still own the place?' Harrison asked. 'I've been away a couple of years. Just come back to see my folks.'

The woman looked sadly at him. 'Ophelia died year before last. So tragic. She was a good woman. Lucas is still here and his nephew, Roger. He manages the place for him.'

'Ophelia died? That's terrible. I hadn't seen her for a long time. Was she ill?'

'No. She didn't socialise much. Never really went off the farm. Didn't need to. She loved it here. He scattered her ashes in their garden. Sad.'

He noticed that she avoided talking about why Ophelia had died.

Harrison got his phone out to pay for the hyacinths.

'Are Lucas or Roger around? Do you know?'

'Don't think Lucas is. Saw his Land Rover drive past the window there, about an hour ago. But you might catch Roger. His house is just down the road on the left.'

'On the main road?'

She nodded and handed him the planter, clearly having

had enough of all the questions. She looked at her watch. That was their conversation ended.

Harrison was about to leave, but turned as though with an afterthought.

'You wouldn't happen to know who the local artist is who makes the terracotta ornaments, would you? I was looking for a robin for my mother.'

The woman looked over to where the display was located.

'What's out is all we have. We won't be getting any more in. They was made by Ophelia.'

Harrison thanked her and left the shop. Another piece of his jigsaw slotting into place.

The sheds, which had been full of workers when he and the DS visited, were now in darkness. Harrison realised that once the shop closed, there would be nobody on site besides Lucas Fry. No one to monitor his activity.

He couldn't go snooping around without a warrant. It would make any evidence he did find inadmissible, and besides, Lucas wouldn't be so stupid as to leave anything lying around. He'd shown just how forensically aware he was. The only slip up had been the music recital ticket.

Harrison was considering driving up to the house to double-check and see if Lucas was in when DS Howard rang his mobile phone.

'Reverend Galloway's gone missing. He's not answering his phone and hasn't turned up to the last two meetings in his diary.'

At that news, Harrison threw caution to the wind and went straight to Lucas Fry's farmhouse. The woman in the shop had been right. He was nowhere to be seen. There wasn't even a dog bark to say that anybody or anything was at home.

Harrison stood contemplating breaking and entering.

The vision of a smiling DCI Turner receiving a complaint from Lucas that when he came back from walking his dog, he found Harrison in his home, held him back. He'd be no use to anyone and certainly not in a position to solve this case if he got himself arrested. Lucas wouldn't have Reverend Galloway here, anyway.

They needed to track down his Land Rover. Try to find where he'd gone.

He had to get back to the incident room and share what he'd found with Detective Superintendent Mark Ferry. If he couldn't persuade the investigation to pivot, then Frank Galloway could be a dead man by the morning.

It was a spur-of-the-moment decision to stop off at Roger Fry's house. From what the woman in the shop had told Harrison, the white house, just set back from the road, must be Roger's. Either way, it was worth a try.

Christmas was very definitely in full evidence at this house. In the sitting-room window, a large tree flashed its merry greeting to passers-by, and a reindeer-shaped frame, covered in white lights, was displayed in their front garden. Harrison reached the front door, where a sign was hanging from it. *Santa Please Stop Here.*

When he knocked, Spud's familiar bark could be heard, accompanied by a cacophony of small excited children. A young man in his thirties came to the door, his leg blocking the exit of Spud and the red-cheeked toddlers behind him.

'Yes?'

'Roger Fry?' Harrison asked.

'That's correct. Who are you?'

Harrison held his police ID card out. 'I'm with the National Crime Agency. I was hoping to speak to your uncle. I don't suppose you know where he's gone, do you?'

'My uncle? No.' A wave of emotions crossed Roger's face.

Harrison could see that his visit had sparked a train of thought.

'Does he usually leave Spud with you?' Harrison asked.

Roger thought a moment, clearly not sure whether what he was about to say next would get his uncle into trouble or help him.

'Why do you need to speak to him?'

'He was helping me with an inquiry. I just wanted to check some information he'd given me.'

'Is he in any danger?'

'That depends, Mr Fry. Are you concerned about something?'

Roger struggled for the right words to say.

'No, he doesn't usually leave Spud. He said he needed to go away for a bit. Wouldn't tell me where. It was unlike him to be so... Well, so clandestine.'

'Do you have keys to his house?'

'Yes.'

'Have you been round?'

'Oh God, no. You're not suggesting he's...'

'No. I don't think he's taken his own life. I just wondered if maybe he'd left some clues as to where he's gone.'

Suddenly, Roger Fry decided that he was talking to a total stranger about his uncle and loyalty kicked in. He had no idea what Harrison's agenda was.

'Well, that's his business – not mine or yours. He's a free man. If he wants to go away for a night or two, then he can. I'll let him know you called and if you don't mind, we have three young children who are all hyper-excited about Christmas and need to have a bath and get to bed.'

'If anything changes, let us know.'

Harrison handed over the business card DS Howard had given him on the first day. There was a hesitation, and the look in Roger's eyes told him he didn't believe everything was alright. Maybe once he'd had a chance to think about it, he might be more prepared to talk.

THERE WAS nothing more that Harrison could do without a warrant, but it was yet more proof that Lucas Fry was up to something, and more than likely, that he had taken Reverend Galloway with him. Question was, where would he have gone?

Back at the incident room, the whole team was dejected. The atmosphere felt like a flat soufflé which had been stamped on by its chef. Totally devoid of any Christmas spirit. It was an air of defeat. Everyone was avoiding the DCI who had been called into a room by Detective Superintendent Mark Ferry and didn't reappear for nearly an hour. He had commandeered the room as a makeshift office and was officially 'assisting' with the inquiry. Unofficially, he was taking control of it.

George had been visited at his home and Reverend Galloway was nowhere in sight. Thanks to Mr Watson, George also had an alibi. He'd come round that afternoon just after Mrs Peterson and Mrs Edwards had left, bringing some cans of beer with him as well as the wreath. Once the Christmas cheer was back up on George's front door, the pair of them had settled in front of his fire to create some of their own cheer.

The result was that DCI Turner's prime suspect was eliminated from the inquiry. They had no leads. No idea of where Reverend Galloway could be.

DS Patrick Howard made a beeline for Harrison. 'We need to go to the boss and tell him what we suspect.'

'The DCI will slaughter you if you go over her head,'

Harrison said. 'Let me do it.'

'No. It's time for me to have my say. She's wrong, and she's protecting him. You know it and I know it. If we don't act now, then I'm going to have Reverend Galloway's death on my conscience.'

'Did you get access to the diocese records?'

'Yes. And it's exactly as we thought, apart from one very important anomaly.'

35

DECEMBER 20TH

Detective Superintendent Mark Ferry listened to Harrison and DS Howard for twenty minutes as they explained their theory of why Lucas Fry was the man they should be looking for. He'd sat with his elbows on the desk, leaning forward and listening intently. Finally, he started to ask them questions.

'So you're telling me that he's gone to all this trouble with these pottery figures, burning down the churches, and the elaborate murders in order to avenge something that happened to his wife years ago?'

'Yes,' Harrison replied succinctly.

Patrick could see that his boss wasn't totally buying it.

'It's to do with symbolism, isn't it Dr Lane?' he prompted Harrison to explain.

'Yes. In Lucas Fry's eyes, these men and the church have been lying. He wanted to highlight the lies of the church, and Christmas in his eyes is a kind of lie. It's almost certainly not Jesus's real birth date, and is instead the usurping of original pagan and Roman celebrations for the solstice.

'The solstice is about celebrating the return of light, the rebirth of the sun. You can see why the Christians thought to link it to Jesus and, as they wanted to convert people from pagans to Christians, it was essential to take on some of the already established sacred dates. Fire is an important component of the pagan celebrations. Lucas Fry is a man of the land. His farm meant everything to him and his wife, and that connection with the land and the weather and sun is what pagans celebrated.'

The DCI concentrated on what Harrison was saying, but furrowed his brow.

'When Lucas found those Roman coins for Saturn on the farm, it must have been a kind of omen for him. His wife is called Ophelia. Saturn's wife was called Op, an easy shortening of his own wife's name. The Roman festival at the time of the solstice and Christmas was Saturnalia, and they gave gifts of pottery figures. His wife made pottery figures which were sold as garden ornaments in their shop. All of these symbols are incredibly important to his state of mind.

'He has entirely justified his actions on the basis of the wrong done to his wife and the lies told by the church. The methods of the murders also back up the fact he is punishing the victims. He flayed Reverend Soulsby to make him atone for his sin. The inside-out crucifixion of Reverend Davenport, religious symbolism and also revenge for the damage I think he believes they did to his wife.'

'I looked at Ophelia Fry's medical records,' Patrick took up the story. 'It wasn't immediately obvious because it's under her maiden name of Preston. But when she was fifteen, she was admitted to the emergency department with severe internal haemorrhaging. She nearly died. In the process, she had to have a hysterectomy. The records state that it looked like a badly undertaken abortion. She refused to say anything and although the police had shown some interest, without her cooperation, there was nothing they could do. There are no formal records of a complaint.'

'I think that incident haunted her for the rest of her life,' Harrison continued. 'She used to be in the choir at St Peter's. Her family were regular churchgoers. That visit to A and E, ties into the time at which she stopped going to church. We believe that at St Peter's church she was raped, or seduced and then Bishop Warriner and the other clergy covered it up.'

'So you think they were all involved somehow?'

'We suspect so. Both men who died were in positions at churches in this area at the time of her admittance to hospital. That was forty years ago. Reverend Davenport had forty nails inside of him. Reverend Soulsby received forty lashes and was made to swallow forty razor blades.'

The detective superintendent collapsed back into his chair and let out a big sigh.

'This is a great theory, both of you. I see the symbolism, but I cannot see any hard evidence against a respected member of this community. If I put resources into tracking down Lucas Fry and it turns out the man has just gone off on a weekend break with his fancy woman, then that could cost Reverend Galloway his life. Plus, your allegations against DCI Turner are extremely serious. I need to speak with the forensics officer that witnessed this hiding of evidence at the scrapyard. Send me everything you have that supports this crazy story of yours and let me consider it.'

HARRISON AND PATRICK walked out of Detective Superintendent Mark Ferry's office and back into the incident room.

'I'm not sure he's buying it,' Patrick said to Harrison.

'I think he's close. But we need a back-up plan. I'm going to go out and look for Lucas. You fight our corner here. We may be too late, but I suspect that dawn is going to be our deadline. If Lucas is following the symbolism to the end, then he's going to wait until the solstice day has dawned. That gives us just a few hours to track them down.'

DCI Turner was watching their every move as they crossed the room to Patrick's desk.

'Watch your back,' Harrison said to him as he picked up his coat. 'Call me if there are any developments.'

HARRISON LEFT the warmth of the small police station and headed out to his car. It felt colder than it had the previous few evenings. The night was still and quiet, sounds still muffled by the snow and the majority of people in their beds.

He looked up at the night sky. It was clear. The snow clouds, at least for now, had moved on. Across the black sky were hundreds of sparkling stars. In today's light-polluted world, he couldn't see half the wonder of the skies, but in the pagan and Roman times, when their only light would have been small campfires and torches, it would have been a wondrous sight. Easy to imagine how insignificant those early people would have felt underneath its canopy. Easy to see how their pagan festivals had meant so much to them.

The moon was a waning crescent shape, the illuminated side pointing eastwards towards where the sun would rise. It would be a weaker winter sun, but when it rose, the crescent moon would disappear in its superior light. If Harrison didn't find Reverend Galloway, he, too, would be gone by sunrise.

. . .

Harrison had sat quietly in his car, clearing his mind and trying to think like Lucas Fry would. Where would he go? Where would be symbolic? What would connect him to his wife? His first thought was the farm. If they weren't at the house, perhaps they were somewhere on their land. Harrison started the engine and headed in the direction of Lucas Fry's farm for the second time that day.

When he arrived at the yard, it was dark except for the security floodlights which were triggered by his car driving through. There were no obvious signs that he was here, so he drove to the house again. The Land Rover was still missing.

He got out of his car and stood in the darkness. Listening. There were no sounds of voices. No shouts for help. Just the cry of a fox from the woods across the road.

Perhaps he was out in the fields, under the big skies like their ancestors would have been. Harrison looked around for a way to get some height. Right now he could do with a drone or heat-seeking helicopter, but until the detective superintendent bought into their theory, he was on his own.

The tallest building on the complex was a grain silo, which loomed into the night sky, its conical roof reaching above all other structures around it. Rising up one side and onto the roof was a metal ladder. If Harrison climbed up that, he would get a view across the fields.

The metal rungs were unbearably freezing cold and so he'd returned to his car to fetch his gloves from the passenger seat. He'd need to be careful the rungs weren't also slippy. There was nobody here to help him.

Harrison climbed slowly up the metal ladder, all the time listening and looking for any signs of life around him. An owl flew close by, the only sound its wings. A ghostly whisper that barely moved the air. He climbed higher towards the black sky, but with each step up the rungs, the only sight he could see was an inky darkness all around. There was no artificial light apart from a glow in a bedroom window of a house at the edge of the fields. Roger Fry's house. Harrison wondered who was up at this time of night.

Finally, he reached as far as he could go. He stopped, looking 360 degrees all around him. Up here the wind was breezier, carrying sounds and smells from miles around. He could hear the distant buzz of cars from the main Lowestoft road a few miles away. The smell of the fir trees which waved at him from across the road. What he couldn't see, hear or smell, was any signs of Lucas Fry and Reverend Galloway.

Harrison descended and headed off to site B on his list, St Peter's church. The site of the original sin. As he drove down the road, he noticed that the light in the bedroom of Roger Fry's house had swapped for one downstairs. Perhaps one of the children was having a bad night, or maybe Roger had been unable to sleep, their conversation earlier playing on his mind.

When Harrison arrived at St Peter's church, the graveyard and building were in total darkness. It didn't look as though there was anybody there, but he got out to check just in case. Nobody had noticed the events at All Saints or St Mary's until the fires had started.

Harrison walked around the graveyard first, looking for any signs of recent activity. He wasn't afraid of being alone with the dead on a dark night. There was far more to fear from the living.

The snow was a big help to him. Its virginal state showed that nobody had gone into the main building via the front entrance, and the only footsteps he could find were those which had led to graves where freshly laid flowers had frozen in the night air.

He scanned the area, taking in the black shadowy shapes

of gravestones and stone carvings to honour the dead. For a moment he thought he'd seen someone, but it was a weeping angel, silhouetted against the moon.

There were no signs of life in the graveyard, and no way that anyone could have gone inside the church, unless they'd flown. The snow couldn't lie.

Harrison looked at his phone. Time was ticking fast. They didn't have long before the sun would start to show itself in the east. He'd not heard from the DS and he was running out of ideas for where Lucas Fry might have gone.

Back in his car, Harrison turned the heating on to full, trying to warm his toes and fingers. He almost missed his phone ringing underneath the full tilt roar of the hot air fan in the car. It was DS Howard.

'Full-scale man hunt for Lucas Fry,' his breathless voice announced. 'Not only did the boss agree to go with our theory, but Roger Fry, Lucas's nephew, just called. He went round his uncle's house and found his will and all his business papers neatly laid out for him. We've got somebody going out to him now. See if we can get any clues as to where Lucas has gone. The boss is calling in the helicopter, armed response is on standby and all officers are going to comb the area. Where are you?'

'I've been to his farm and St Peter's church. There's no sign of them.'

'OK. If I get anything more, I'll let you know.'

Harrison collapsed back into the seat and turned the heating down. Where were they? His mind went to Lucas Fry's house and imagined Roger turning up and finding his uncle's will and the paperwork. Flashes of their meeting with Lucas went through his mind. The painting of the house with the ghostly image of him and his wife at the front door. The coins. The photographs on the wall.

That was it. The photographs on the wall. There were several of the same place. Ness Point, Patrick had said. It was where people went to watch the sun rise. What was symbolic about the solstice? The sun. So, what would you do on a solstice? You'd go to the most easterly point where you'd be sure to see it. Lucas and his wife had gone there many times, probably one of the few visits she'd been happy to undertake, as there would have been so few people around.

Harrison texted DS Howard to tell him where he was heading and pointed his car towards Lowestoft.

36

DECEMBER 21ST

For such a symbolic place – the most easterly point of the United Kingdom – Ness Point had a fairly disappointing ambience. Consisting mostly of concrete and tarmac, the most visible landmark was a huge white wind turbine. In the darkness, its massive blades rose high into the sky and slowly turned through the air like a strange, other-worldly creature. For a moment Harrison wondered if that was Lucas Fry's destination, but he quickly dismissed it. Instead, he followed a sign which pointed along a wide concrete walkway to the Euroscope and Ness Point itself.

The waves splashed against the sea wall, sending their salty spray into the air. It was still almost completely dark, but as he walked, Harrison could see the expanse of the horizon begin to widen before him. Here they would be the first in the United Kingdom to see the sun rise across the sea on solstice day.

As he neared the point, Harrison became aware of a shape up ahead. It looked too tall to be a human. He approached silently, trying to keep away from the sea wall where his silhouette would be easier to spot.

Then, around twenty yards away, a figure stood up from the floor.

'Hello, Dr Lane. I had a small bet with myself that it would be you who turned up to the party first.'

Harrison stopped in his tracks. He couldn't see his face – he was just a shadowed outline against the sea behind, lit only by the weak light of the moon. But he knew the voice.

Behind him was a large circular shape on the floor: the Euroscope, with a big cross on top. Harrison strained to see what was attached to it. As his eyes adjusted and his brain worked overtime to piece together the shapes, he realised he was looking at Reverend Galloway, tied to the wooden cross on some kind of stand. The rotted corpse of Bishop Warriner, still wearing his robes, was tied onto the cross with Galloway.

'Come any closer and he'll die immediately. I've covered them in diesel,' Lucas Fry warned.

Harrison stayed where he was standing and discreetly dialled DS Howard's number.

'I thought you'd worked it out when you came round the house. All those questions about Saturnalia. But you know it's fine now. Lynne Turner did her job of slowing down the investigation. Bet you struggled to get anyone to believe you. Do they even know now or are they still harassing poor George?'

'They know it's you, Lucas,' Harrison said pointedly, knowing full well that DS Howard had picked up.

'I can see your phone, Dr Lane. Please, don't hold back, call the team. The more the merrier. I want this to be a party. The plan was to wait until some of the photographers and solstice worshippers turned up to watch the sunrise. They'd have called the police then. You've just stolen their thunder, that's all.'

Harrison put his phone to his ear. 'Did you get that, Patrick?'

'Yes. On my way, as are armed response and the helicopter. Keep him talking.'

Harrison didn't end the call. He left the line open so that the DS could listen in.

'This has been for Ophelia, hasn't it?' Harrison asked. He knew that Lucas would be keen to talk about his wife.

Lucas took a few deep breaths and looked out to sea.

'You never met her, so you have no idea what a wonderful woman she was. There wasn't a bad bone in her body. Yet she spent her life feeling like she was evil and worthless. No matter how much love I gave her and how much I told her she wasn't.'

'What happened to her?'

'This devil. Traitor to his religion and all the people he professed to serve. He raped her. She was just fifteen years old. And it wasn't just the once. Her parents trusted him. They let him into their home when she said she felt too ill to go to church. They allowed her abuser into her bedroom. Nowhere was safe. She thought it was her fault. He told her she was a temptress and that it was her who had brought this on them both. Like Eve had done to Adam.

'And then she became pregnant. He panicked and went to Bishop Warriner. Another Judas who, instead of helping Ophelia and casting Frank Galloway from the Church, hid his sin. He asked Martin Soulsby and Edward Davenport to take her for a secret abortion.' Lucas stopped. His throat had become so tight with the emotion of his story that he could no longer get the words out. This was the first time he'd spoken them aloud. Released them from his conscience and his heart.

'Do you know how much pain she went through when they butchered her insides? She nearly bled to death, and there was nothing left for her to create life again. That broke her. And it stole from us the chance to have a family of our own. But that pain was only a part of it.

'They told her that what happened was her punishment. That she had tempted Reverend Galloway, and it was her who had brought all this on herself. Every day of her life she carried that burden of guilt and no matter what I said to her, no matter how much she grew to hate what they had done to that fifteen-year-old girl, she could never shake that shame.'

Harrison heard the sound of helicopter rotor blades approaching and from further back in the car park, vehicles arriving.

Lucas Fry continued with his story, as if oblivious.

'Yes, what I did to Soulsby and Davenport was evil, but it was payback for what they'd done to her. They took her to the backstreet abortionist. They dragged her into that butcher without her parents' knowledge and without her consent. Then they just dropped her off at her parents' house, where she nearly bled to death, and they never once mentioned it again.

'They lied for forty years. Covering up the truth. Never admitting to the sins that had been committed. Do you know how hard it was to enter into their churches and be civil to those men when I knew what hypocrites they were? And this man, he raped my wife when she was just fifteen years old. A child. He allowed her to be butchered just to save his own reputation.'

Harrison looked to where Reverend Galloway was tied to

the wooden cross. His mouth was gagged, but his eyes were open, wide with fear. He tried to shake his head desperately.

'I see your friends have arrived,' Lucas said, and he reached into his pocket and drew out a lighter. He bent down to pick up an object on the floor and Harrison realised it was a fire torch, just as it burst into flame.

'Wait!' he said desperately. 'Did Ophelia tell you it was Reverend Galloway?'

'No. She couldn't even bear to write his name down. That's how much pain it still brought to her. I had a chat with Soulsby and Davenport in order to get that information.'

'They named Reverend Galloway?'

'Soulsby said it was the vicar of St Peter's.'

Harrison gave a small nod. 'I'm sorry for what happened to Ophelia. But you have the wrong man, Lucas. Reverend Galloway is innocent. Forty years ago, when your wife was being abused, he was having his tonsils removed. The church records show that he was on six months' sick leave. They brought in a locum vicar. He was a favourite of Bishop Warriner's and went on to rise up the church ranks. He also went on to abuse other young women.

'That man, Edgar Lawson, is currently in prison after being found guilty of several counts of rape and unlawful sex with minors. He is the man who should be tied to that cross, not Reverend Galloway. You are about to kill an innocent man.'

'You're lying.'

'I'm not. There's a copy of the church records on my phone. I can show you.'

Harrison held out his phone.

Lucas Fry seemed to fold in half at his words. The fight leaving him.

Harrison could hear the police radios behind him giving

instructions in the marksmen's ear pieces. Getting them into position.

'DCI Turner worked out it was you, didn't she?'

'Yes. I'd been so careful, but I must have had that damned recital ticket in my coat pocket or somewhere. When it was found at the scrapyard, she knew.'

'Did you tell her about your brain tumour?' Harrison asked. He wasn't sure he was right about this suspicion, but his conversation with Dr Oliver Charles and what he'd witnessed of Lucas's symptoms, gave him enough to think it worth the question.

'Oh, you are a clever one, aren't you? How did you work that out? No, I didn't tell her. She thought we were going to be together. Had a future.'

Behind him, Harrison heard a small sound like a wounded animal. He guessed that DCI Lynne Turner had arrived and heard everything he'd just said.

'I didn't tell Ops either. I went to the hospital appointments, and I never told her what I was doing and why. She thought I was having an affair. That I'd grown tired of her. Lynne Turner put that thought in her head. She kept coming round, making Ops think that there was something going on when there wasn't. Told me she'd been in love with me since our school days.

'Ever since she'd got her promotion, the visits started. She seemed to think it would impress me, make me leave Ops for her. I despised her. It has always been my wife I loved. Never anyone else. I was trying to protect her by not telling her about my brain tumour. It's inoperable, you know. She was so fragile. Instead, I lost her and that woman was the catalyst to her fatal depression. Lynne Turner hid evidence to protect me. I hope she loses her career for that. It's the only other thing she's ever cared about.'

Harrison gave him a moment before speaking again. 'Can you let Reverend Galloway go now, Lucas? I promise you that he has done nothing to hurt you or your wife.'

Behind Lucas, Harrison could just see the first orange line appear on the horizon as the sun started its climb into the sky.

Lucas Fry began to cry. Huge fat tears rolled down his face and his body shook with the effort of the emotions he'd been holding in.

'This has to end tonight, Dr Lane. I don't want to die a slow, painful death, ballooning on steroids and enduring everyone's pity when they look at me. I certainly don't want to do that from a jail cell. There's nothing left to live for. Roger will take care of the farm.'

Lucas glanced at the rising sun and then turned towards the cross, holding the flaming torch.

'It's time,' he said and took a step towards where Reverend Galloway was struggling to free himself. He looked as though he were offering the flaming torch to his victim.

Harrison heard the command on their radios. The instantaneous shot as the marksman took Lucas down. He was propelled backwards, the flaming torch flying out of his hand and landing just a couple of feet away from the diesel-drenched cross.

For a few seconds, it was as though time stood still. Lucas lay prostrate on the floor. All Harrison had eyes for was the torch, which had begun to roll slowly towards the cross.

Harrison had already anticipated this. He knew that Lucas wanted to die. Why else this public show? If he'd simply wanted Reverend Galloway dead, then he'd have done it somewhere private, as he'd done with the others. He'd wanted the armed response team there. The trouble was, they didn't realise just how flammable the cross and

Reverend Galloway were. By shooting Lucas, they were endangering his victim.

Harrison had already assessed the cross and the vicar's position. There would be no way to get him down and free, and be able to put out the flames quickly, if the torch touched them. If Galloway survived the fire at all, he'd be badly burned.

When he heard the order to shoot, Harrison leaped forwards. He had nothing to lose. There were just seconds to save Frank Galloway from a painful death.

He flung himself, rugby tackle-like, at the torch as it continued its slow roll towards the base of the cross. His hand reached out and grabbed it, pulling it up and away from the floor and then throwing it towards the railings where the sea reached up to swallow its flames.

As he came to rest on the ground, Harrison looked behind and saw that Reverend Galloway was safe. The cross was unlit. Beside him was Lucas Fry, blood pooling from the gunshot wound and from the back of his head where he'd cracked his skull on impact.

Harrison was sure he'd changed his mind. He wasn't going to light the cross. The good man in him won through. He didn't want to make a victim of an innocent man. But he had wanted the marksmen to think he was going to do it.

He got his wish. His dead eyes stared ahead at the rising sun, which they would never again witness.

37

DECEMBER 21ST

Diving onto concrete hadn't come without pain, but once the paramedics had realised that most of the blood on Harrison's clothing was from Lucas Fry, they agreed that he was fit and didn't need to go to the hospital. He'd grazed his palms, knees, and elbows, but he'd survive.

Reverend Galloway was a different matter. He was in a state of extreme shock, having been kept locked up with the corpse of Bishop Warriner before being doused in diesel and expecting to die in flames.

Detective Superintendent Mark Ferry couldn't thank Harrison enough, and the beaming smile on DS Howard's face was a reward in itself. The icing on the cake was the sight of DCI Turner being taken away in a police car.

Harrison was hugely relieved that the case was over and he could return home, but his euphoria was tempered when he looked at his phone. He hadn't seen the text message at first, not until after the medics had given him the all clear. It was from the DCI before she was taken away for questioning.

They're watching. Was all it said.

For anyone who might look at her phone, it could have been a harmless message to tell Harrison that the rest of the team were there with him and watching Lucas Fry. But he knew better. He knew exactly what she meant and although it made his stomach tighten and reminded him of the struggles he had ahead, it also strengthened his resolve. *They* were not going to stop him from finding out the truth.

38

Ryan hadn't exactly enjoyed being locked inside a metal reinforced cardboard wardrobe, but he'd quickly recovered when he discovered where he'd been taken. It was like having been away on an awful trip and then waking up to find yourself in a sanctuary.

Harrison's apartment was bigger than he'd imagined. The only issue was the massive window overlooking the Thames, which sent his agoraphobia into overdrive. The window didn't possess any curtains or blinds and so he'd had to walk through the apartment to the spare bedroom with his head turned away from it, looking at the faces of wizened Native Americans and their artwork instead.

Calvin had been a godsend. Eventually all Ryan's belongings from the flat had arrived, and he'd constructed a small wall of boxes at the end of the open-plan kitchen and sitting area allowing Ryan to go into the kitchen, and even sit down on a sofa, without seeing the window. It wasn't exactly going to win any interior design awards, but it would ensure that

Ryan could at least get some food and relax while he was there.

The fridge was conspicuously empty and so Calvin had also gone out to the shops to get in some supplies for him. Ryan rooted around his kitchen box for 'proper' tea bags and coffee, not the herbal stuff. By the time Calvin returned with milk, they were both able to sit down and drink a decent cup of tea.

The adventure and the several nights of anxiety and little sleep had taken their toll on Ryan. He was still asleep in bed the next day, when he heard the front door of the flat close and footsteps walk across the wooden floorboards.

For a few moments, he laid still, eyes wide open, paralysed with fear. His mind groggy from sleep and nightmares. Then Harrison called out to him.

'Ryan?'

He jumped out of bed in seconds, relief propelling him forward.

The sight of Harrison made him stop in his tracks.

'Holy crap, what happened to you?' Ryan said, looking at his boss who was variously patterned with blood, torn clothes, and dirt.

'Been a busy morning,' Harrison replied, smiling at his assistant with relief. 'What's going on with the great wall?' He nodded towards the barricade of boxes.

'You seen that window of yours?' Ryan said to him.

'Ah, sorry. Forgot about that. But glad you've made yourself at home. I'm going to have to be unsociable. Need a shower and sleep. Let's catch up in a few hours.'

'No worries. You look like you need it.'

. . .

IF HE COULDN'T HELP Harrison by doing some work, Ryan decided instead to repay him with a good meal. He knew that his boss didn't really cook – it was always either ready-made meals, takeaways, or big salads. By the time Harrison woke up at 6 p.m. that evening, the flat was filled with the delicious smells of a roast dinner.

Harrison appeared heavy-eyed and proceeded to look stunned at the domestic scene in front of him.

'You don't have to do this, you know,' he said to Ryan, who was serving up roast potatoes and beef. 'But it looks great. I'm starving.'

Ryan smiled to himself. 'It's not just snacking I like. You don't get my figure without knowing how to cook a good meal.'

'We can get you onto my treadmill while you're here,' Harrison replied.

'Err... I think I'm allergic. Go all dizzy on those things.'

Harrison winked at him. Ryan breathed a sigh of relief.

'So, everything went smoothly with the move?' Harrison asked.

'Yeah. Calvin sure knows his stuff. Where did you find him?'

'He helps at the Taekwondo club with me. He also does Krav Maga, the Israeli martial art – it's a military-grade practical fighting and defence system. He runs a bodyguard and security business. Not much that man doesn't know how to deal with.'

'I'm very grateful. Thank you.'

'Just sorry it came to that. We need to be more careful with the next place.'

'Calvin said Addie and his gang were arrested?'

'Yeah, the plan was to get them inside the building for the police to arrive. The police are looking for a rival gang behind it. Jack doesn't know anything about Calvin and he can't find out. It would compromise him. He made sure the armed response unit was ready to jump in, but that's as far as his involvement goes. This way, Addie's gang doesn't know you've got links to the police.'

Ryan nodded and finished his last roast potato.

'What's the plan for the next few days?'

'Christmas shopping and lots of sleep,' Harrison said. 'We're taking a break.'

39

CHRISTMAS DAY

If Harrison was struggling with the fact that he woke up in his flat with two other people in it on Christmas morning, then he didn't show it. The man who enjoyed his own space and didn't celebrate Christmas had breakfast with two of the most important people in his life: Ryan and Tanya.

Admittedly, the great wall of boxes was a fixture which would eventually begin to niggle, but after a few beers, Ryan had started to create a mural on it with a fake River Thames scene. It had made Harrison smile, especially as he'd watched Ryan and Tanya add cartoon characters to it the previous night, giggling at who could make the most ridiculous scene. He'd put up with the boxes if it meant he had Ryan in a safe place and under his protection.

As for Tanya, she'd come over for Christmas Eve and helped massage his sore knees, which had taken the brunt of the landing on the decidedly hard concrete Euroscope. Being with her brought a warm sense of peace into his life.

With the flat door closed, he could shut out the rest of the world, the murders, his past, the people who didn't want him to find out the truth about his mother's death. He blocked it all out and was determined that for a few days at least, he would rest and spend time with the important people in his life.

Tanya had insisted on bringing over a fake Christmas tree, complete with baubles and flashing lights. 'I'm not spending Christmas without any decorations,' she'd said to Harrison – and he'd reluctantly acquiesced.

A hamper of luxury food had been delivered on Christmas Eve, with a note of thanks from Reverend Frank Galloway, his family, and the church. Harrison had let Ryan unpack it, enjoying listening to the murmurs of joy that each extravagant food item elicited.

Harrison had already been to the supermarket, battling the crowds and huge checkout queues and with strict instructions to get everything that was on the list compiled by Ryan and Tanya – not the meagre standard items that he'd have bought. Consequently, his fridge and cupboards were fuller than he'd ever seen them and he wondered how they were going to get through that amount of food. He needn't have worried. By the morning Ryan had done a good job at denting the stock already.

Christmas morning, they bagged up all their gifts that Tanya had insisted were put under the tree the night before. One remained.

'Are you going to take that one, Ryan?' Tanya asked.

'It's for my mum,' he said, throwing a glance at Harrison.

'She's back?'

Ryan nodded.

'We can always drop in on the way home – if you want?' Harrison said quietly.

'I'm not sure... Maybe another day.'

. . .

Jack and Maria had made a huge effort, decorating the house and ensuring that they had absolutely everything their guests would want on Christmas Day. Tanya played with baby Daniel while their hosts finished up the lunch. Ryan had forced Harrison to have a game of *Mastermind*, and then totally regretted the choice of game when his boss was able to guess where the coloured pegs were placed within a few moves by watching Ryan's body language.

Just before lunch, they all sat down and shared their gifts.

Harrison had been on tenterhooks. It was the first time he'd bought presents like this and he'd spent many hours agonising over his choices.

Jack and Maria were delighted by the weekend in a luxury hotel near to where her parents live in East Anglia. That meant they could leave baby Daniel with her mum and dad and spend a couple of nights on their own. Harrison knew the full story about Maria's postnatal depression and Jack's warm embrace when he thanked him was worth every penny.

Ryan was like a child when he opened his present and found a photograph of a top-of-the-range gaming chair.

'It was too big to bring on Christmas Day, but it's on order and should be here in time for your new flat,' Harrison explained.

Ryan beamed back.

For Tanya, he had bought the one thing that they'd both been craving for and not been able to have. Time together.

'It's a long weekend in a Spa hotel in the country, with nothing to do but walk, eat and be together,' he whispered to her.

She'd looked up into his eyes and kissed him so tenderly he thought his heart might burst.

'It's perfect,' she said.

'And I promise I will not answer any emails or phone calls.'

'I will be holding you to that,' she teased back.

Christmas lunch took the rest of the afternoon. They had turkey, pigs in blankets, roast potatoes, sprouts with chestnuts and bacon, carrots and parsnips in honey, and stuffing, plus lots more.

They pulled their crackers and Harrison had even put the paper hat on – although it was a little small for his head and he declined any photographs to mark the moment.

Once the main course was finally over, Harrison helped Jack to take the plates out into the kitchen. Their speaker was playing Christmas music and Jack returned to the dinner table singing 'The Holly and the Ivy'.

'Come on you lot, we should be singing Christmas carols,' he'd said, laughing and bursting into a rendition of 'We Three Kings of Orient Are'.

'You know that barely any of this has anything to do with the Christmas you think we're celebrating,' Harrison had said to him. 'It's mostly pagan originally. The holly and ivy, the yule log, and, of course, the date itself. I won't get started about Father Christmas.'

Jack stopped and looked at him with his eyebrows raised. 'Does it matter?'

Harrison looked around him at the laughing faces of the people he cared most about in the world.

'No,' he replied.

At that moment, Marie walked back in with the Christmas pudding.

'Harrison, I hope you don't mind a bit of brandy on the pud?' she said. 'It mostly burns off, anyway.'

'I think that's fine.'

'We don't want you getting tipsy and trying to arm wrestle us,' Jack joked with him.

Harrison watched as Marie put a lighter to the pudding, and blue flames leaped across its surface. For a brief moment, he was taken back to Suffolk. The burnt churches, the frightened face of Reverend Galloway tied to a cross with the corpse of Bishop Warriner. He thought of DCI Turner's spiteful look as she'd compared him to the estranged father he despised, and maligned the mother he had loved and whose death he would never stop trying to avenge. Then he pushed those images from his mind and focused on those he was with, celebrating life. He looked around the table at the people who weren't blood relatives, but were the best family he could have ever hoped for.

'Merry Christmas,' he said to them all, raising his glass of apple juice.

'And let's hope next year is a good one,' Jack added. 'Cheers.'

Ryan and Harrison exchanged a quick glance. One thing they both knew for sure: it would undoubtedly be another busy one.

A LETTER FROM THE AUTHOR

Thank you for reading *Winter Graves*, I hope you enjoyed the latest instalment of Harrison Lane's investigations. I certainly enjoyed coming up with some bizarre methods for Lucas to dispatch his victims, I'm a nice person really! Please if you get the opportunity, I would appreciate you leaving a review and welcome any feedback you'd like to share with me on my social pages, or via my website. If you want to join other readers in hearing all about my new releases and bonus content:

www.stormpublishing.co/gwyn-bennett

Thanks also to the fantastic team at Storm Publishing for helping to get this book into your hands and for putting their faith in Harrison. My publisher, Kathryn Taussig; editor, Natasha Hodgson; proofreader, Nicky Lovick; cover designer Tash Webber; all the amazing support staff like Melissa Boyce-Hurd who keep the engine running; and of course the man at the helm, Oliver Rhodes.

If you would like to read a free novella, telling the story of how Harrison and Ryan first set up the Ritualistic Behavioural Crime unit, please pop on over to my website www.gwynbennett.com. Please also connect with me and join in the conversation on my and Storm Publishing's social media platforms.

I hope you will continue the journey with Harrison. He's off to a forest in book 8 where his unique talents will again be very much needed.

Until next time, happy reading,
Gwyn Bennett

www.ingramcontent.com/pod-product-compliance
Lightning Source LLC
Chambersburg PA
CBHW011035190726
48290CB00011B/2859